The Knitting Circle
Rapist Annihilation Squad

Derrick Jensen
&
Stephanie McMillan

Cover and interior design by Stephanie McMillan
Edited by Theresa Noll

10 9 8 7 6 5 4 3 2 1

ISBN 978-1-60486-596-7
LCCN 2012913620

PM Press
PO Box 23912
Oakland, CA 94623
www.pmpress.org

Flashpoint Press
PO Box 903
Crescent City, CA 95531
www.flashpointpress.com

Printed in the USA on recycled paper, by the
Employee Owners of Thomson-Shore in Dexter, Michigan.
www.thomsonshore.com

Like the patch on the cover?
Order one for $6 (5 for $25) from
derrickjensen.org or stephaniemcmillan.org

The Knitting Circle
Rapist Annihilation Squad

Derrick Jensen
&
Stephanie McMillan

CHAPTER 1

Marilyn never ceases to feel happy when she talks with her students about rape. Most have never heard the word, and even when she spends hours talking about its history, her students have difficulty grasping the concept.

Sometime during the discussion a boy always says, "But if I did something like that, the girl wouldn't want to be my friend."

Marilyn smiles and nods, encouraging him to say more, but invariably he just shakes his head.

And later a girl always asks, "So how did people stop rape for good?"

Marilyn smiles and nods again: it's time to tell them about the great knitting needle revolution.

"It all began," she says, "with my mother's best friend, Brigitte. She didn't set out to be a revolutionary. She just wanted to make some fabulous sweaters."

An attractively plump, middle-aged woman greets the bus driver as she boards, shakes out her thick red hair, and settles on her seat. She wears a colorful flowered dress more suited to a cruise ship than to this city bus. The driver eyes her pretty pink shoes and finds them entirely too cheerful for these mean and gritty urban streets. He prays their owner takes care to protect them from sidewalk hazards, such as sticky wads of used gum, and the vile juices of discarded hamburger wrappers and gnawed chicken bones.

Oblivious to his concern, the woman pulls knitting needles, yarn, and a half-finished sweater from her tote bag and gets to work.

This is my godmother, and my dear friend, the soon-to-be-revolutionary Brigitte.

That afternoon Brigitte had received a phone call from her new dance instructor inviting her to a special midnight class for advanced students. She almost refused—it was a long haul on the bus—but then he told her he would be teaching a very special set of moves called the Caterpillar Transformation Dance.

That changed everything. She'd recently seen a documentary about this dance and its amazing chakra-recalibrating effects, and her chakras were definitely in need of recalibration. She heard destiny calling.

As she knits on her way to the dance studio, Brigitte hums a lively tune, quietly enough that she doesn't annoy the other bus passengers. Not that it's humanly possible to hum loud enough to be heard over the mob celebrating the city's victory in the National Chess Championship. Riding home after an evening of rioting, setting small yet well-designed fires in dumpsters, and overturning police cars, the nerds howl with grape soda–induced laughter as they reenact their most impressive chess moves. One hops two seats back and one over to represent an especially exhilarating knight maneuver.

The other passengers are all regulars. There are the exhausted slaves going home from the swing shift, dreading their unhappy spouses and cranky, tired children. There are the people who ride the bus purely for the air-conditioning, back and forth, back and forth, all day and all night long, to escape the hellish heat outside. There's the pair of teenagers making out a few rows ahead of Brigitte, who become frantic when they simultaneously realize their stop is next and discover their braces are locked together. There are the two teenage boys playing "clear the seats," a game that involves each hiking up one butt cheek, holding that position, then high-fiving his comrade as other passengers scatter. Brigitte is grateful the boys are seated a fair distance from herself.

Too close, however—in fact, directly in front of her—sit a man and a woman. The woman asks over and over, at full volume, "Just tell me, do you love her?" and the man hisses back, "We'll talk about it later." This goes on for blocks. Finally Brigitte can tolerate it no longer. She taps the man on the shoulder. "Tell her already—we all want to know!" The other passengers lean forward, waiting for his answer. He claims he does not, but a straw poll indicates most passengers do not believe him.

Then of course there are the obligatory boys playing Dungeons & Dragons, the three radicals in the back plotting to overthrow the government, a young woman practicing her tennis serves down the aisle, and a group of trained Navy SEALS balancing balls on their noses. When a priest, a rabbi, an imam, a Lutheran minister, and a polytheistic pagan sorceress board the bus and approach the overhead bar, Brigitte decides it's time to get off.

Looking out the window, Brigitte realizes that leaving the crowded bus may be even more disagreeable than the ride has been. This neighborhood is cruddy enough during the day, but it's positively menacing at night. Many of the streetlights aren't working, and few pedestrians are about.

She almost decides to turn around and go home. A lurid thriller she's eager to read, *The Everglades Avenger*, waits on her nightstand. But she pulls the cord to signal the driver to stop.

"Now, you take care of those pretty shoes, ma'am," he says as she makes her way down the steps.

Brigitte walks along a darkened sidewalk, swinging her tote bag and still humming. She glances behind her to make sure no one is following. (Marilyn's students are never able to understand someone having to do anything of this sort.) She adopts the walk that all women from an early age learn to use in scary places: rapid, firm, and purposeful. Look like you are determined to get where you're going, and are eagerly awaited by many large, aggressive friends who will scour the earth searching for you if you don't arrive promptly. Appear confident. Show no fear.

The street is deserted. The buildings Brigitte passes are miserable boxes fronted with weeds struggling to break through the concrete. Bedraggled hand-lettered signs scream desperation and failure: "Moved to www.secondhandcutlery.com." "New management—we don't suck like they did!" "Buy one, get thirty-seven free!" A faded poster slumps in a window, "90% off retail price! This weekend only!"

She steps in gum. Damn it.

Finally, she sees the neon sign ahead, a weakly glowing magenta heart announcing the safety of the dance studio.

The cavernous dance studio is dimly lit by candles lining

the edges of the polished wood floor. Their flames reflect and multiply in the mirrors along the walls. Romantic music plays, and it takes Brigitte a moment to recognize the end of Barry Manilow's "Mandy." There is a pause before the next song begins, a medley of Manilow's advertising jingles. She hears Manilow sing, "C'mon, get a bucket of chicken, have a barrel of fun."

She stops humming and softly calls, "Hello? Hello?"

Riversong de la Huerta, the dance instructor, steps into the candlelight. (He tells everyone his New-Age name means Riversong of the Heart, but it actually means Riversong of the Market Garden. He serenely ignores all helpful souls who attempt to inform him of his error.) Tall and handsome, he owns an impressive head of shiny black hair and a magnificent mustache he calls "the mane of a lion on the face of a lover." His shoulders are draped with gauzy colorful scarves. He wears a eurotard (20 percent more Lycra), a wide leather belt, and knee-high black leather boots.

"Hello, pretty one," he calls as he strides across the room.

Brigitte looks around, confused. "Where is everybody? You said there was a class tonight."

Riversong's voice rumbas from somewhere behind his glorious mustache: "It's a very special class. For me and you."

Brigitte frowns. "I'm leaving. I don't appreciate—"

"I've been watching you, Brigitte. The way you move. Your grace. Your subtlety. Your lithosity."

Brigitte blinks twice. "I'm fifty-three years old. I haven't been lithe for thirty years." She blinks again. "Well, fifteen."

"Do you know French, Brigitte?

"No."

"Ah, too bad. You have that certain something the French call, '*Je bande comme un ane et meme les plus de la classe m'ont le dos.*'[1] And so, as they say in Paris, '*J'ai carrément besoin de faire mon trou et toi, t'es toute mimi.*'[2] Or as they say in Marseille, '*Faute de grives, on mange des merles.*'"[3]

Brigitte puts her hands on her hips. "And all of this means?"

Riversong answers, "It means you are ripe for the Caterpillar Transformation Dance, where the little caterpillar grows and grows, becomes fuller and fuller, until he bursts forth to fly away as a butterfly."

Brigitte nearly leaves in disgust. But then she remembers the testimonials in the documentary. She really needs her chakras recalibrated. And she's come all this way on the bus.

"Hell, I'm here. Let's give it a shot." She drops her tote bag and walks toward him.

Riversong stands tall, arms outstretched, the scarves draped over his hands. "With these silk scarves we give the caterpillars wings. Like so!" He moves his arms in circles. It's actually quite pretty and impressive.

He hands the scarves to Brigitte. She tries. It looks okay, but not stunning.

Riversong and his extraordinary mustache implore, "Lose yourself, Brigitte! Drop your inhibitions!"

Brigitte tries again. She's still not very good.

"Let me show you." He moves behind her and takes her wrists in his hands. He guides her arms in the proper motions: big circles, grand gestures, sweeping scarves.

Brigitte stops suddenly and pulls away. "Is grinding your

---

1 Translation: I'm horny as a toad in heat, and even the vulnerable young ones in class have turned down my sexual advances.

2 Translation: I need a confidence-builder something fierce. And you're not half bad.

3 Translation: When one can't find quails, one eats crows.

hips part of the choreography?"

"Oh, yes! It's all part of unleashing your butterfly!"

"Well, I can feel your caterpillar, and I don't like it."

Riversong leans to her ear and says softly, beseechingly, "My caterpillar needs to be in a cocoon. Your soft, warm cocoon."

"What?"

"Your butterfly needs to spread her wings. Let's fly together!"

Brigitte laughs. "Riversong, I could never be attracted to someone who mixes metaphors."

He says earnestly, "My love knows no grammar. I want you."

"When I was a little girl," she responds, "I wanted a pink pony. I didn't get that either. I'm flattered, kind of, but I'm leaving now."

Riversong spins her around and pulls her body against his.

She pushes him away and starts walking toward the door. She hears him behind her and walks faster, then begins to run. He chases her around the mirror-lined room, into the prop room, and back out to the dance floor. The scarves around his neck flap furiously behind him. He reaches out and almost catches her, but she slips away. Finally he corners her near the front door and shoves her against a wall.

She struggles in his arms and says, "Stop it this instant!"

He and his mustache say together, "Never! I listen only to la Huerta! Listen to your heart, Brigitte! Your mouth says *no*, but your la Huerta says *oui, oui!*"

"No. My whole body is saying *no*. No, Riversong, no."

"It takes more than mere words to stop this runaway freight train of love." He reaches down and pulls a ridiculously bejeweled dagger from his boot. It looks like a souvenir from

Disney World, but it's sharp. He points it at her, and she can tell he knows how to use it.

"You're not leaving," he says.

Brigitte stares at him a long time, then asks, "Is that how you want it?"

His mustache hides the movement of his lips as he says, "No, my dear, that's how you want it."

"I'm not choosing this."

"Yes, you are."

"This means that much to you? This is how you want it?"

"This is how I'll take it."

Brigitte looks down. She sees her tote bag on the floor slightly behind him and to one side. The top is open, and the knitting needles are barely visible. "So you're going to take it?" she says.

"Oh, yes."

He kisses her forcibly. After a moment she stops struggling and reluctantly puts her arms around her assailant.[4] Riversong

---

4 "This is the moment," Marilyn tells her students, "when the whole story turns. If this story were being told not by Brigitte or me or someone like us, but rather by Riversong or by others like him" — and here she lists off a whole string of writers and filmmakers, people like Nabokov, Miller, Lean, Kazan — "the point of the story would not be Brigitte's resistance, or how awful rape is, but rather how the woman actually wanted the man the whole time."

Her students are inevitably befuddled by this insanity. To exemplify this insanity in storytelling emphases and purposes, she contrasts, for example, the rape scenes in *Dr. Zhivago* or *Straw Dogs* — where the woman starts by repelling the man's violent advances, but in the end pulls him close, showing that's what she wanted all along — with the rape scene in *Deliverance*, where because it is a man and not a woman being raped, the rape is not romanticized or trivialized or made to be just another form of foreplay, but rather is shown to be humiliating, violent, and violating. At no point does Ned Beatty's character pull the rapist closer, nor whisper that he loves him.

closes his eyes in ecstasy, murmurs, "Much better. You like, no?"

Tightening her grip on Riversong, Brigitte stretches out her right leg and uses her toe to snag the handles of her bag on the floor behind him. She raises it with her foot, reaches around him with her left hand to get inside, and pulls out a knitting needle. Riversong gyrates against her, delighted with the apparently enthusiastic contact. With a sudden scream and a move reminiscent of *Dial M for Murder* (she, being a rabid fan of classic film, cannot help but notice), she stabs him.

His eyes widen in disbelief. The leonine mustache twitches its final twitch. That is all. Well, perhaps a final gurgling noise or two, which are over quickly and barely worth mentioning. Riversong falls, a knitting needle piercing his la Huerta.

Brigitte stands over Riversong's body and looks at it impassively for a few moments. She sighs. "No, Riversong. I no like."

She tugs the knitting needle from his body, wipes the blood onto one of his scarves, and slides the needle back into her tote bag. She walks to the door and uses another scarf to wipe her fingerprints from the knob and then to turn it. She peers out, looks both ways, and lets the door click shut behind her before walking briskly back to the bus stop.

Brigitte wearily enters her house, closes and locks the door, flicks on a light, and tosses her tote bag onto a chair. She sighs heavily and sinks onto the couch, then suddenly leaps up to race to the window and scan in both directions before firmly shutting the curtains. She paces back and forth, unsure what to do.

In the bathroom, Brigitte looks in the mirror and sees tears forming in the eyes of the woman in the glass. She blinks them away, forces her face to relax. She keeps looking. Slowly her mouth begins to form a smile.

She walks back to her living room, sits down, and dials a number on the phone.

"Nick," she whispers.

Nick cheerfully replies, "Why are you whispering? Do you have a special guest?"

Brigitte whispers, "Why am I whispering?" Then she says in a normal voice, "No reason. Why indeed? What are you doing?"

"You caught me at a very busy time. I'm choosing between watching *Gone with the Wind* for the twenty-sixth time or *Casablanca* for the thirty-fourth."

"Come over. I can do better than that."

"Better than Rhett and his ill-fitting dentures? Better than the thrill when Ingrid Bergman says, 'Kiss me. Kiss me as if it were the last time'?"

"Better than both; I guarantee. I've had a rough day. Please come and take my mind off my troubles."

"What happened, sweetheart?"

"No discussions, honey. It's something I can't think about right now. If I do I'll go . . ."

They say together, ". . . crazy. I'll think about that tomorrow."

They both laugh.

Brigitte says, "What I need right now is distraction."

Nick says, "So that you can forget for one night that the problems of a few little people don't amount to . . ."

They say together, ". . . a hill of beans in this crazy world."

They both laugh again.

"Sit tight, Brigitte," Nick says. "I'll be right over."

Nick hangs up the phone and starts to get dressed, strutting around as he hums Hot Chocolate's "You Sexy Thing."

He spritzes cologne into the air and walks through the mist. He combs his hair, smiling at himself in the mirror. He looks down at his crotch and says, "Big Louie, if Brigitte and I weren't already such good friends, I'd say this is the beginning of a beautiful friendship."

Meanwhile, Brigitte sits with her hand on the phone, half-smiling, humming the same song. She stands, changes her clothes, then brushes her hair.

At first Brigitte didn't tell anyone, not even Nick, what she had done. For weeks she was terrified the police would arrest her, but Riversong had, for obvious reasons, made no record of her visit that night. Brigitte was never visited by the police, much less questioned. She carried on with her life as usual.

The next step in the revolution took place several months later. It was accompanied by the smell of cheese. Smoked mozzarella, to be exact.

Every Thursday night Brigitte and five other women gather in the back room of a cheese factory for their knitting circle meetings, not to plan revolution, but rather to talk and knit and plan their next group trip to Daisy's Craft Barn to pick out more yarn. They started meeting at the cheese factory because it was the only appropriate public space they could find that would let them use a room for free.

A couple of years before, they had met for a time in a back room at a rescue center for cats, but even though they were all animal lovers, they found that the smell of cat urine began to permeate their yarn. And who wants to wear a sweater that smells of pee?

After that they met for a few months in the basement of

a fundamentalist church. That tenancy had ended one evening when one of the church elders just happened to be kneeling outside one of the doors to their meeting room, and just happened to have his ear pressed against the door when Marilyn, fourteen at the time and not normally a member of the group, asked Brigitte why she'd never had any children.

Brigitte responded that she'd never wanted any, and so she had taken great care to always use various forms of protection, which she would be delighted to describe in detail and recommend or disrecommend to Marilyn if she was in need of such information.

Red-faced and mortified, Marilyn said of course she didn't have any *need* for it. She was just curious. But had Brigitte's protection ever failed?

Brigitte said, "Yes, once."

"What happened?"

"I ran down to Baby-B-Gone faster than you can say, 'Not every ejaculation deserves a name.'"

The eavesdropping elder, unable to contain his righteous fury, burst into the room and banished the evil women from his church.

After that they heard of a Satanist church offering a free room for use. Since they were just going to knit anyway, they didn't much care what sort of church it was, so long as it had a free room. But when they arrived for their first meeting at the "church," they found it was in fact a sixteen-year-old-boy's basement in his parents' home, "complete" with black light, black bean-bag chairs, and the boy's original drawings of Led Zeppelin posters. When the boy said they looked best under black light, Brigitte wondered, but was kind enough not to say in his presence, if they wouldn't look even better under no light at all. After that came a succession of dusty back rooms behind failed storefronts: wedding stores that seemed to fail as often as the marriages themselves; a second-hand store started by someone who'd lost her job in the failing economy and who thought it might be a brilliant idea to reopen a second-hand store started by someone else who'd lost her job because of the economy and who then lost the second-hand store; and a small, dirty, noisy room behind a chocolate factory. They put up with the crowding, the filth on the floor, the spider bites, and even the occasional fright by a rat in exchange for their ability to spend a few hours a week swimming in the smell of pharmaceutical grade chocolate: one week dark, the next week milk, and semisweet the week after that. But even chocolate couldn't help them rationalize staying after they overheard the owner yelling at his daughter for a bookkeeping mistake, calling her stupid, and then hitting her. He kicked them out after they turned him in to the police.

When the room at the cheese factory became available, the members of the knitting circle, still leery after the unfortunate cat pee fiasco, were concerned that their sweaters would smell like cheese. But they had nowhere else to go. Happily, the cheesy fragrance didn't seem to permeate the yarn too awful much. The only even remotely cheese-associated consequence of knitting in this room was that they all unaccountably seemed to make friends more easily with dogs, cats, and people from France.

This week the factory smells like smoked mozzarella. Brigitte is sitting next to her best friend Gina, the mother of Marilyn. In spite of, or perhaps because of, Gina's long-time closeness with the flamboyant Brigitte, she normally dresses as her opposite (in a style she terms *sensible* and Brigitte silently labels *dowdy*; of course she is far too polite and kind to ever say this aloud). Mary, an avid gardener, favors floppy hats. Christine is famous for neatness. It is rumored she can walk through a hurricane with not one hair out of place, not because of hair spray, but from sheer force of will. And the youngest members, in their early twenties, are Jasmine and Suzie. Inseparable, these two friends nearly blind passersby with sparkle, glitter, and embellishments, from their metallic hair scrunchies to their iridescent eye shadow to the tips of their rhinestone-adorned toenails.

On this particular day, although everyone else talks happily about food, clothes, crazy relatives, politics, and so on, Mary is silent. So silent that it becomes impossible to miss. Finally, Suzie asks what's wrong.

Mary stops knitting, sits still a moment, as if deciding whether to say what she is thinking, and then says, "I'm sorry. It's just . . . my granddaughter was raped a couple of days ago."

There is a moment of stunned horror, before the room fills with expressions of condolence. Oh my god! No! How terrible! Goodness! How is she?

Mary says, "As you'd expect. You know."

"Poor thing. How awful. Oh, no," everyone murmurs.

Brigitte asks, "Who did it?"

"The counselor at her high school."

All faces harden. Knitting needles click very fast.

Christine says, "No!"

"That's where I went to school. I could always tell he was a creep. I could just tell," says Suzie.

Jasmine shakes her head. "I thought he seemed nice."

"Just because he fools some people, doesn't mean he's not a rapist," Brigitte says.

Gina nods. "Don't I know that one!"

To which Mary replies, "You, too?"

"Not that 'nice' guy, but another."

Christine looks at her, her face soft. "Gina, you've been raped, too?"

"*Too*? You mean you were?"

Christine nods, lips pressed together. They each put down their knitting, get up, hug briefly, then return to their chairs.

They knit quietly for a few moments before Jasmine says, "The guy who did it to me seemed nice, too. At first."

"Mine never bothered to pretend," says Suzie.

Mary stops knitting. "Nor mine."

Gina glances from once face to the next, her brow furrowed. "Wait, have we all. . . ?"

Silence. They all look at each other, appalled as each hesitantly raises her hand. After a moment they slowly resume their knitting.

Gina says, "It was my cousin."

Suzie, "A cop."

Mary, "My abusive ex-husband."

Jasmine, "My ex-boyfriend."

Christine, "My prom date. That was a long time ago. Later it was a priest."

Brigitte, "A country-western singer. Afterwards he even wrote a song about it."

The room is silent except for the clacking of knitting needles.

Christine turns to Mary and asks, "Will your granddaughter go to the cops?"

"Cops won't do anything. They never do," Mary says.

Jasmine asks, "Never?"

Gina snorts in derision. "Did they in your case? Rapists never get what they deserve."

"Who do you call when the one who did it *is* a cop?" asks Suzie.

No sound except for the needles.

Suzie says, "Anybody in this room whose rapist went to jail, raise your hand."

All knitting stops. They look at each other. No one raises her hand. Knitting resumes.

Gina says, "I used to work at a rape crisis center. Guess what percentage of rapists spend even one night in jail."

Jasmine says, "Half?"

Gina snorts again, "Try six percent. They almost always get away with it."

Christine shakes her head. "That's just not right. Somebody needs to do something!"

Suzie shakes her head, too. "Good luck. That will never happen."

No one speaks while they knit.

Another group of women might have let it drop there. Another conversation might have ended the way so many conversations like this end—*somebody should do something, but nobody ever will, and that's a sad fact of life, so let's adjust to it the best we can.*

The women knit quietly for several minutes. Then Suzie says, "My mom always tells me if you want to get something done right, you've got to do it yourself."

The clicking of needles stops as they digest this. Brigitte smiles to herself. The clicking resumes.

Christine hesitates before saying thoughtfully, "I read a book about village life in China under Mao, right after the revolution. Women formed patrol groups, and when they saw a man beating a woman they dragged him out of the house and beat him up. If he was caught doing it again they increased the punishment. Wife-beating stopped very quickly."

The women let their knitting fall to their laps. Only Brigitte keeps knitting calmly, smiling.

Christine continues, "And more recently, the Gulabi Gang in India has been doing the same thing. Can you imagine several hundred women in pink saris chasing men who beat women?"

The women smile broadly.

Jasmine asks Christine, "What do they do when they catch them?"

"Well, they don't give them candy kisses, I'll tell you that much. Oh, and they also beat police who steal from or falsely accuse the poor."

"That's the coolest thing ever," Jasmine says.

"Why don't we ever take justice into our own hands like that?" Suzie says.

The women stare at the walls, the ceiling, the floor, a few inches to the side of each other—anywhere but into each other's eyes.

Finally, Brigitte says, "Um. I did."

The women look at her in shock.

Christine gets a sly look in her face and says, "Spill it, sister."

Brigitte spills the story of stopping her mustachioed attacker.

Suzie asks, "Weren't you scared?"

"Of course. That's why I did it."

Jasmine asks, "Do you think you might get caught?"

Brigitte looks at each of them and says, "Not if you don't tell."

They both use their knitting needles to cross their hearts. Everyone else in the room nods grimly.

Finally, Suzie begins to giggle. When everyone looks at her she asks, "What did you do with the weapon? Are you using it right now?"

Gina sputters, "That's disgusting!"

Everyone stares at her.

She explains, "It had his blood on it. Who knows what nasty disease she could have caught!"

They laugh, all except Gina, who digs in her purse for an alcohol wipe, then gingerly takes Brigitte's knitting needles and sterilizes them before returning them to her.

Suzie pantomimes putting needles on her head, says, "She could have mounted his head on the wall, with two knitting needles for antlers."

Jasmine catches the fever: "We could all become big game hunters!"

Suzie: "Have a contest!"

Jasmine: "Go on safaris!"

Suzie: "Issue licenses and set bag limits!"

Gina stops laughing and says sharply, "No!"

"Absolutely not," says Brigitte, in an even stronger tone.

Everyone looks at them, wonders why they're spoiling the fun.

Gina says, "No licenses. No bag limits."

Brigitte adds, "It's got to be open season."

Everyone laughs. Knitting resumes.

Finally, Gina asks, "So what are we going to do about that school counselor?"

CHAPTER 2

A couple of weeks later, Mary is in her kitchen mixing green enchilada sauce into ground beef for meatloaf. Her second husband, Theodore, is in the living room watching the "Believe-It-Or-Not Super-Thrill-Filled News-O-Tainment Hour." She half listens as the newscaster details the latest tabloid-style spectacles: "Mother asks police to handcuff her five-year-old child and send him to the pokey! Believe it or not! Two middle school students were caught having sex in class! Believe it or not! Miss USA contestant almost stumbles on her gown! Believe it or not!"

Then she hears something that makes her pay attention: "Police have reported that James Noggle, counselor at Westwood High School, was found dead today in his office. He had been stabbed in the heart with a knitting needle. There are no suspects as yet! Believe it or not!"

Mary smiles and whispers, "Thank you, Christine."

A few nights later, Suzie is in her family's living room with her parents and her nine-year-old brother. He's an okay brother, except that he still picks his nose. That is what he is doing with intense concentration as the newscaster announces, "Police have reported a second bizarre knitting needle murder. Todd Kurz, a decorated police officer, was stabbed in the line of duty last night. The following photo of the crime scene is graphic, and viewer discretion is advised. Please send all kiddies, puppies, sentimentalists, Hallmark card enthusiasts, and for entirely other reasons, communist sympathizers from the room. Or at least cover their eyes."

Suzie's father says to her little brother, "You heard him, Bub."

Finger still in nose, her little brother replies, "I'm not a comminis simpa-sizer."

Her mother reaches to cover his eyes. He removes his finger long enough to push away her hand. She wipes her own hand on a handkerchief she keeps ready for this very reason.

The television plays soft and tasteful yet still toe-tapping patriotic music—kind of like John Phillips Sousa on Valium. The photo that appears on the screen shows a police officer sitting in his patrol car, dead, a box of doughnuts and a bondage porn magazine by his side and a knitting needle stuck through his heart. A doughnut hangs from the needle.

Suzie smiles and whispers, "Thank you, Jasmine."

Her mother says, "What did you say, dear?"

"Oh, nothing, Mother."

Her little brother removes his finger, stares at it a moment, then puts it back in his nose.

A few nights later, Christine sits up in bed, where she's under her covers eating chocolate-covered ginger bits and watching television.

The newscaster says, "The knitting needle murderer, clearly now on a killing spree, has struck for a third time. Police report that an elderly gentleman, Enver Alcatraz, was found dead in his home dressed in an ill-fitting tuxedo. He was stabbed with a knitting needle right through his boutonniere, which was composed of red carnations. Police also report that when he was found, he was clutching a corsage, and his CD player was still playing Neil Sedaka's 'Happy Birthday Sweet Sixteen.' The dance card of Mr. Alcatraz has, sadly, been punched for the last time."

Christine raises her chocolate in a toast. "Ha! Thank you, Gina!"

The next week, a man sits alone on a wooden chair in the center of a large living room in a small mansion. The walls are decorated with paintings of cowboys at work and photograph after photograph after photograph of women—some beautiful, some not so, some young, some not so, some dressed, some not so—posing with the man now sitting in the chair. In the photographs the man always wears a cowboy hat. Now he wears that same hat, long white underpants, and boots with spurs. A guitar rests across his lap.

His handlebar mustache is perky. His hat rests at a jaunty (yet practiced) angle. His spurs would still jangle if he could move his feet. But he is dead. A knitting needle protrudes from each ear. Trails of blood congeal on his neck.

One of his songs plays on the turntable (although he'd put out a couple of dozen CDs, he was a purist to the end and owned only a record player):

> *My baby, she didn't say yes*
> *But she didn't say no.*
> *A little hankyspanky*
> *And she was a-ready to go.*
> *Stolen kisses are sweeter than gold*
> *And stolen sexy-wexy*
> *It never gets old.*

The song reaches its end and so does the LP. Since there is no one there to turn it off, the record player makes a repeated clicking sound as the needle bumps against the end of the record. Chuk. Chuk. Chuk.

Fans of this country western singer pack a church for his funeral. Most wear all-black western-style outfits bespangled with sequins. The jangles of spurs sound like hundreds of tiny bells helping to wing the man's soul to heaven, or to some other place. Black cowboy hats are removed one by one as mourners enter the church and approach the casket, where they admire its carvings of horses and guitars, horses playing guitars, and men playing with horses. Inside the casket is the singer, now fully dressed, with his mustache even more personable and miraculous than that of the now-forgotten Riversong.

Several women from the knitting circle are also in attendance. They are not wearing black, but bright pink. And they're knitting. As they wait for the service to start, the clicking of their needles echoes in the cavernous holy space.

The priest has not yet arrived.

Time passes, and though the mourners want to pay their respects to their beloved troubadour, they also have meetings to attend, dogs to walk, partners to have sex with, people to e-mail, and in some cases special friends with whom they will combine the sex and e-mail. But the priest still fails to arrive. People begin to check their watches. Some send text messages. A few pull out laptops. A few of these make extra sure that no one else can see their screens.

Finally a deacon emerges from a back room and approaches the pulpit. He wipes the sweat from his face with an embroidered hanky. He clears his throat nervously, says, "My deepest apologies. We can't seem to locate the, um, priest. In the meantime, since the deceased was a singer, why don't we all, um, sing a hymn? Does anyone have a suggestion?"

One of the women in pink suggests a hymn of thanksgiving. Others, including many not wearing pink, snicker.

The deacon disguises his own laugh with a cough, then says, "Ahem, why don't we start with 'Abide with Me'? Lenny, can you lead the mourners in song?"

Lenny, a young man who also works in the church, makes his way to the pulpit. He walks awkwardly, as though with every step closer to having to face the audience, he withdraws further inside of himself. His uncombed, slightly greasy hair falls a little more over his face with every step. By the time he gets to the pulpit his hair shields his eyes entirely. It would be easy to laugh at his eccentricities if it weren't painfully clear they were a symptom of some trauma. Standing as far as possible from the microphone, he begins to softly sing—chant would be a better word, and whisper would be even better than that. Most of the mourners join him, though without much enthusiasm. Some continue to text. A few look around furtively, then stare all the more intently at their laptop screens. The deacon retreats again into a back room.

Alone, he mutters to himself, "Where the hell is he? And where did he move the wine? If I'm going to be stuck leading this damn service, I'm sure as hell going to need a shot of the blood of Christ."

The deacon rummages around in cabinets, looking for the wine. At last he opens the largest cabinet of all. Out tumbles the body of the priest, pierced with a knitting needle.

The voice of the deacon echoes throughout the church: "Holy fuck!"

The priest's funeral takes place several days later, and is even grander than the singer's. The church is packed with flower arrangements, wreaths, mourners, and a small contingent of women wearing pink.

The deacon is in the pulpit, and he intones somberly to the audience, to the air, and to God Himself, "Remember, Lord, those who have died, and especially remember Father Luke, whom You have called to You from this life. In baptism and holy orders he died with Christ; may he also share His resurrection."

The mourners respond, "Amen."

The deacon says, "Father Luke was a great man. We sure will miss him."

The mourners mumble, "Amen."

The deacon looks around, scratches the side of his head, and then says, "Oh, who are we kidding? He wasn't great; he was a monster! No one's going to miss him—it's a day of great rejoicing! Let me hear a Hallelujah!"

Lenny is the first to respond, "Hallelujah!"

The audience roars, "Hallelujah!"

The deacon says, "Thank you, Lord, for punishing Father Luke for all his filthy deeds! Thank you, Jesus!"

The audience responds, "Hallelujah!"

Lenny shakes his hair out of his face and pumps his fist in the air, his hallelujah soaring higher than any other.

Later, many call it the best funeral they've ever attended, and a YouTube video of it goes viral, getting more hits even than "Chipmunks Gone Wild," "The 100 Greatest Movie Insults of All Time," "Dance Your Way to Hot, Sexy Abs," and the previous number one all-time blockbuster hit, "Skateboarder Hits His Nuts on a Pole."

Picture a television. The frame is slim, but the screen is wide and tall, and it covers the entire corner where it lives, where it dispenses wisdom, where, like the ancient elders, it gathers the young to tell them stories that teach them how to be human beings (or in this case, how not to be human beings). But that corner of the room is more than just a gathering place to receive profound lessons and guidance. It is a place of worship, where this digital god receives its due, its daily offerings of time and attention, where it accepts the gladly given souls of its supplicants, and gives them in return *Lars and the Real Girl*, *Paris Hilton's British Best Friend*, *Hostel*, *Everybody Loves Raymond*, and the *Evening News*.

The television is on. Like the computer, like the omniscient and all-wise God it is and has become to so many, it never sleeps. And like a good neighbor it is always there. But to many it is more than a neighbor. It is their family and friend and lover and priest and therapist and lullaby singer and dreamweaver. It is their mother's breast and father's shoulder, their lover's body and confessor's ear. And always—*always*—it speaks to them, tells them how and what to think, tells them what is wisdom and what is folly, tells them whom to trust—*trust me*, it says, *put your trust in me*—and tells them whom to fear.

The television is on. It shows its supplicants fast-moving computer graphics with higher definition than the human eye can perceive. Some of its acolytes say it shows higher definition than life itself. Blasphemers say this is nonsense, that life isn't digital; it's infinitely complex. Members of the techno-television priesthood reply, "Your lips move, but I can't hear what you are saying."

The television is on. Images of knitting needles fly rapidly back and forth across the screen. Red letters dripping blood flash like an alarm. They read, "The Hunt is on for the Knitting Needle Killer." A single chord in a minor key clues the viewers to feel terror, fear, anxiety, discomfort, or failing all of those, at least some minor indigestion. Then, mood set, the graphics dissolve to show Franz Maihem, a tall, slender man, messianic, looking almost exactly like Jesus the Christ, except that he's Germanic and not Semitic, shaven instead of bearded, short-blond-haired instead of long-black-haired, and he's neither hanging on a cross nor handing out loaves and fishes, but rather striding purposefully down an office hallway. But in all other ways he does look very messianic, in a television drama sort of way.

He stops, faces the camera, and says laconically, "It all began with that most trusted of figures, a high school counselor. Who would want to do him harm? What sort of monster would pierce the heart of such an innocent man?"

A searching glance lets members of his congregation know that they, too, should ask the question: Who could do such an awful thing?

"Next came a police officer. A protector. A knight in shining blue armor. Who will protect us when our protectors cannot be protected?"

Another searching glance. Among the faithful, spines shiver and hair stands on end.

"Then an old man wearing a tuxedo. Who could be more benign than that? If this killer will harm an old man in a tuxedo, an old man listening to Neil Sedaka, who can be safe?"

This time, hairs shiver and spines stand on end.

"Then an entertainer, and now a priest. This killer has shown that nothing is sacred to him, not even country and western music."

A pregnant pause, which Franz knows precisely when to

abort. He opens a door in the hallway. The scene shifts to show a man sitting behind a desk. He looks almost exactly like Franz, except that he is tall instead of short, slender instead of plump, bald instead of blonde, and brown instead of pink.

Franz says, "With us in Catastrophe Studios is FBI agent Chet Stirling, here to shed light on what sort of monster could commit the horrible murders of so many innocent victims. Chet?"

Chet speaks. His voice is precisely like that of Jesus, except that we don't really know what Jesus sounded like. And Chet speaks English instead of Aramaic. But he does sound very messianic, in a technician-Christ sort of way. He says, "Thank you, Franz. Using the most advanced scientific methods and our decades of experience, we've put together a profile of the killer."

Chet holds up a drawing of a generic face: a circle with dots for eyes and a straight line for a mouth. He continues, "We're probably dealing with a white male in his thirties, who, while slightly antisocial, remains a good neighbor, except that there might be reports in the area of the occasional disappearing cat. He may work as a postal carrier or a circus clown. We suspect his mother was a scary bitch who beat him with knitting needles. His victims, ranging from a country singer to a police officer to a priest, are clearly random . . ."

The women of the knitting circle gather for their regular meeting at the cheese factory. Today is provolone.

Gina says to the group, "We've got a problem."

Christine asks, "Oh, are you still having those dreams where you have to roll a great round of Muenster cheese up a steep hill of scalloped potatoes?"

"No. The problem is way worse. Did you see the news last

night? They're clearly not getting the message."

Brigitte responds, "Yes, I did see! They gave credit to a man!"

Mary answers, "No surprise there. When don't they?"

"And they said it was random!" Brigitte is outraged.

Gina says, "We can't stop rape if no one knows why these guys were killed. We have to make the message simple so it can be absorbed by their simple little minds." She pulls disposable rubber gloves from her purse (she *always* keeps disposable rubber gloves in her purse; don't you?), puts them on, and picks a piece of paper from the middle of a stack. She writes in big black letters: "Stop rape or face the wrath of the Knitting Circle."

The television is on. Franz is back, still messianic though still looking like nothing so much as a television news host. He asks Chet for the latest updates on the investigation of these horrifying crimes.

Chet tells him, and tells all of the worshipers, "The FBI has received a so-called communiqué claiming credit for the murders. It's from a group called The Insane Terrorist Bitches Knitting Circle."

Franz is aghast (or at least feigns aghastment): "They actually call themselves that?"

"I'm sure you understand that for security reasons we cannot discuss that particular topic."

Franz recovers from his feigned aghastedness enough to ask, "Has this group made any demands, or are the killings as senseless as they seem?"

"We feel it prudent to not reveal the content of this message."

"Why is that?"

"Our expert analysis shows that these are impersonators trying to steal the glory of the real murderer. We have no wish to reward these lonely women with the attention they so clearly crave."

Gina's kitchen looks precisely how you would expect the kitchen of someone who is both sensible (would her friend Brigitte say "drab"? Certainly not out loud) and germ-phobic to look. She doesn't go so far as to have a paper towel dispenser—this would be germ-phobic but not environmentally sensible—but nor do dirty dishes last longer than a minute—to leave them just a teensy bit longer might sometimes be sensible but would certainly not be germ-phobic. The hand- and dishtowels (sensible cloth in dowdy tans and blues) are washed frequently—maybe less often than linen at five-star hotels, though she hopes more often than linen at Big Al's Buy the Hour Motel.

Gina sits with her husband Lawrence at their sensible tan wood kitchen table drinking weak tea. She takes his hand in hers and says, "I have something to tell you."

Lawrence looks up mildly. "What is it, dear?"

"It's very serious."

"Oh no. You're not ill, are you?"

"No, I'm fine."

"It's not Marilyn, is it? Is she sick?"

"Our daughter's fine."

"Your mother?"

"No."

"Your sister?"

"No."

"Your—"

"Nobody's sick, Lawrence."

"What a relief!" He withdraws his hand from hers and picks up his cup.

There is silence for a moment before Gina says, "Somebody's dead."

Lawrence puts his cup back down. "Oh, no! Marilyn?"

"I said she's fine."

"Your mother?"

"No."

"Your sister?"

"No."

"Your—"

"No," she says. "Someone we don't personally know."

"Oh, well, whew. That's good, isn't it? Or bad. Or . . . wait. How does this relate to us?"

"I killed someone."

"Oh my god, what happened? A car wreck? Are you okay?"

"It wasn't an accident. I murdered someone."

"Are you serious? What? Who?"

"No one I knew. No one important."

Lawrence, the sensible husband of his sensible wife, sensibly asks, "Why?"

"He was a rapist. He raped a friend of mine."

Lawrence is silent for a while before he says, "Oh. Hmm. Well. That's all right then." He pauses a moment before asking the next sensible question: "You didn't leave any fingerprints or other evidence, did you?"

Chet is on the TV again, wearing the look of certainty that signals ironclad job security. He reports, "We now believe several copycat killers have begun emulating the knitting needle killer. According to our FBI expert profiler—"

Franz interjects, "That's you, right?"

Chet nods humbly, then continues, "The copycat killers are most likely white males in their thirties, slightly antisocial . . ."

It's artichoke-flavored cheese week at the cheese factory, and Brigitte is steaming. She pounds her fist on the table in the center of the room. "It's an outrage how serial killers are constantly stereotyped in the media!"

Christine shakes her head. "Tsk. Antisocial white men indeed. Of all the nerve."

Gina comments, sensibly, "The media always distort the truth."

Suzie responds, "I guess we'll have to take our message straight to the people."

"How do we do that?" Jasmine asks.

"We'll have to be direct," suggests Gina.

"Yet sneaky," adds Brigitte.

Gina's walk-in closet in the bedroom she shares with Lawrence looks as you would expect: clothes neatly organized by color, and within color by shade. But there's an additional layer of organization, too, with fabrics sorted by their "friendliness with germs," as Gina puts it. Those most friendly are kept in back for use only when circumstances demand, and the fabrics who don't so much like germs are at the ready for everyday use.

Gina stands in the closet's doorway. She says to herself, "Sneaky?" A moment's pause, then, "Sneaky."

She walks briskly into the closet and finds the appropriate articles of clothing. A few minutes later she emerges wearing a black scarf, hat, sunglasses, hooded jacket, and a burglar's mask.

She looks in a mirror. She says to her reflection, "Too much?"

The reflection says back, "Too much."

When she next exits the closet she is wearing simple yet elegant black pants, a black turtleneck, and a knitted black cap.

The doorbell rings.

Gina bustles down the stairs and opens the door.

Brigitte is standing outside wearing an all-black burglar's outfit with sunglasses and a mask. The only thing missing is a black bag labeled *Swag*.

Marilyn, who is at this point sixteen years old, walks from the living room into the entry way. She looks at her mother and Brigitte, then curls her lip in a way that evolution has made possible only for teenagers.

"What the hell?" she asks in a tone of appalled scorn.

Gina asks, "What?"

"Why are you dressed like that?"

Gina says, "Funeral."

Brigitte talks over her, "Costume party."

Gina corrects herself. "Costume party."

Brigitte talks over her, "Funeral."

Marilyn, sensible daughter of her sensible mother, says, "You're up to something. I can tell. Something weird."

Gina looks her daughter straight in the face and says, "I have no idea what you're talking about."

Brigitte grabs Gina's arm to pull her out the door. "Come on, Gina, we're late for the poetry reading."

Marilyn looks at them suspiciously. "I thought you said it was a funeral."

To which Brigitte responds, "You ever been to a poetry reading?"

Marilyn stalks back into the living room and confronts her father. "Mom's writing poetry now?" she wails, deeply upset.

"Welllllll . . ."

Marilyn softens and puts her hand on his shoulder sympathetically. "I've heard that every marriage has rough spots. You guys love each other. Poetry doesn't have to mean the end. Do you think she'd agree to counseling?"

"Umm . . ."

Marilyn says, "Dad, you need to insist."

The members of the knitting circle meet at a dark, deserted parking lot behind a boarded-up factory. Because none of these women were until recently routine breakers of the law, they all wear the ridiculously overdone burglar outfits of amateurs, with black berets and ski masks, sunglasses, black scarves, and black gloves. Jasmine even wears black mittens (which she knitted herself). When the other women look askance at them, she cries, "They were all I had!"

Suzie smiles and says, "And look how well they match her shoes!"

Christine passes each woman a stack of leaflets. The women split into pairs, return to their vehicles, and drive to prearranged target areas to post their leaflets, which bear a simple message in black ink printed on red paper: "STOP RAPE OR FACE THE WRATH OF THE KNITTING CIRCLE."

Gina and Brigitte drive to a residential district and park in a shadowed space two blocks from a supermarket. They skulk to the edge of the supermarket's parking lot, where Gina staples a leaflet onto a telephone pole.

Brigitte stage whispers to her, "You can't put that there!"

Gina responds, "We've killed people, and you're worried

about telephone company regulations?"

Brigitte says, "It's not that." She rips off the flyer and points to the one underneath. "You were going to cover up a poster about a lost puppy. People will think we're heartless and cruel."

"They already think we're insane terrorist bitches."

"But what about the puppy?"

Gina searches for a better spot. The telephone pole is covered with other flyers announcing a lost kitten, a lost ferret, a lost pig, and a lost scorpion who "answers to the name Hank."

Brigitte points to an advertisement for a diet plan. "Here. Cover this one up."

Gina looks at it. "Diet plans. Ugh. Self-hatred in a box."

"Plus the meals taste like crap."

"And the servings are too small."

The television is on. Chet speaks with the certainty of one who knows that being an expert is like being a bank executive, in that it means you never have to say you're sorry: "Eyewitness tips combined with our careful analysis indicates that the so-called 'Knitting Needle Killers' may not be knitters after all, but may instead be using knitting needles as a clever ruse to throw law enforcement off track. Our latest theory is that these serial killers are actually bad poets.

"Please note that their possible status as poets does not diminish their danger to society. We are advising all citizens to avoid coffee houses, independent bookstores, and most especially, any venue advertising an 'open mic.'"

Suzie and Jasmine sit in a coffee shop. Three long lines of tired young men and women snake across the room and out the door. The people's faces are pale, their eyes half-lidded. At the head of the first line a woman hands over a wad of cash, and says, her voice and body shaking, "Hit me hard, will you?" The barista loads a cup with coffee sludge so thick she has to try twice to force in a spoon. Suzie and Jasmine politely look away while the woman takes her first hit, and when they look at her again, she is no longer shaking. She straightens. Her eyes brighten. The second line is for the more serious junkies; here they dispense with the cup and the sludge and snort straight powdered coffee beans (although at some of the lesser establishments the blow is cut with other, weaker stimulants, like cocaine). The third line leads to a small booth where an RB (registered barista) sits each customer down, adroitly draws up a sleeve, applies a tourniquet, finds a vein, slips in a needle, and helps the customer mainline 100 percent pure Colombian.

Suzie and Jasmine, only recreational users, are sipping coffee and nibbling brownies. Each has her computer open in front of her. Suzie's computer is smaller than Jasmine's, which is in turn smaller than Suzie's, which is of course slightly smaller than Jasmine's.

Suzie says, "Analog propaganda never works. Time to get serious."

Jasmine responds, "Blogging phasers engaged."

"Bomb every forum!"

"Activate text networks!"

Suzie and Jasmine begin typing furiously.

On TV that night, Chet speaks with the certainty of one who has never been unemployed. He says, "We now believe that the group of killers is based in Nigeria, and is funded primarily by the widow of a reputable Nigerian banking official who has been transferring money to the bank accounts of trusted accomplices."

The Knitting Circle does not rely solely on digital propaganda, but continues to spread the word in the physical world.

Picture this: Mary and Christine perch precariously atop the fencing on a pedestrian highway overpass. They hang a banner that's visible to the speeding cars below. It reads: "STOP RAPE OR FACE THE WRATH OF THE KNITTING CIRCLE."

Or picture this: A train pulls up to a crowded metro rail platform. On the side of the train graffiti reads: "STOP RAPE OR FACE THE WRATH OF THE KNITTING CIRCLE."

Or picture this: Mary, wearing her floppy hat, pilots a small plane. People standing on the street look up to see writing in the sky: "STOP RAPE OR . . ."

And picture this: You are standing in front of city hall. Flowerbeds have been planted such that the peonies and chrysanthemums spell out: "STOP RAPE OR FACE THE WRATH OF THE KNITTING CIRCLE."

CHAPTER 3

And so the Knitting Circle Rapist Annihilation movement burst onto the sociopolitical scene with the force of a ripe watermelon hurled from an apartment-complex roof onto a summer sidewalk.

Everyone suddenly clamored to be part of it. Some joined for the cachet. Some joined for the glory. Most joined to kill rapists. With the strength of a powerful movement behind them, women refused to take any more abuse.

Picture this: a taxi stops at a curb. A woman pays and tips the taxi driver, then exits the car. She begins to walk through a city park. She appears cheerful, swinging her handbag jauntily, smiling at passersby.

She smiles at a man sitting on a bench. He flicks his tongue at her suggestively. She frowns. He stands and grabs his crotch. He demands, "Come over here and suck my dick!"

The woman, angry now, stops and stares at him. Then she says, "You talkin' to me? You talkin' to me? You talkin' to me?" She looks around, then back at the man. She continues, "Then who the hell else you talkin' to? You talkin' to me? Well, I'm the only one here. Who the fuck else do you think you're talkin' to? Oh yeah? Okay."

She pulls knitting needles out of her sleeve. He backs off, terrified. She smiles and steps toward him.

It is mascarpone week at the cheese factory, and the air smells as sweet as the breath of baby hummingbirds. The six original knitting club members circle the table, but this week they are not alone. Women pack every available bit of floor space in the room. Outside the door, the crowd spills onto the street.

The next day, Brigitte and Nick share a table at a café. The café is empty in a three-o'clock-in-the-afternoon-and-we're-not-in-a-trendy-part-of-town-and-our-business-is-barely-holding-on sort of way, and Brigitte and Nick are sitting there being eyed by a waiter in an I-wish-they'd-buy-more-since-they've-been-sitting-there-for-so-long-but-nobody-else-needs-the-table-and-I've-seen-them-before-and-they-tip-well-so-I'll-keep-going-over-to-see-if-they-need-anything sort of way. Brigitte is finishing a piece of tiramisu. Nick is sipping water with lemon. In front of him is some untouched cannoli.

He says, "You must take me with you to the knitting circle."

"What knitting circle?"

"Don't play coy with me, Brigitte."

"I don't play coy," Brigitte says coyly. "Do I feign modesty? Yes. Am I coquettish? You bet. But I never play coy." She bats her eyelashes.

Nick continues, "I think I know what's going on, and I want to help. I share the wrath!"

"Do I look like a wrathful woman to you, Nick?"

"Please bring me to a meeting!"

"Since when have you been interested in knitting?"

"Since it became so much more than scarves and sweaters. I want to do something meaningful."

"And meet women."

"Of course. But for that I could have joined the knitting circle any time. Right now I also want to make a difference. I want to help."

Brigitte says, "You're being so serious I hardly recognize you. There's more melodrama here than in *Gone with the Wind*."

"You know I'm the man for the job," Nick says.

"I'm not sure any man is the man for this job."

"Ah. So you admit you're up to something?"

"I admit nothing more than that if you're not going to eat your cannoli, I want it."

"You're not going to give in, are you?" Nick says.

Brigitte responds, "Not yet. I have to maintain my reputation for coyness."

Brigitte and Gina walk toward the cheese factory. They can tell from blocks away this will be a stinky cheese day, already detecting the delicate scent of overripe durian mixing with stale onion and even more stale sweat socks. They can also tell from the wrinkled noses of the crowd milling outside.

Brigitte sighs. "I'm having a problem with Nick."

"I'm sorry. What's wrong?" Gina responds.

"He wants to join the knitting circle."

Gina bursts out, "That's great!" Then she stops walking, thinks, says, "Isn't that great? Oh. It's not great?"

"Definitely not great. I don't want him to."

"Why not?"

"I'm afraid it's going to destabilize our relationship. Or rather, our beautiful nonrelationship. I love the guy; he's awesome. He's fun. But I don't want him invading my life."

"Would it necessarily mean that?"

"We have a great thing going. It's strictly limited. We hang out. We watch movies. We laugh. We have fabulous sex. But that's it. We don't have endless boring conversations analyzing our feelings. We don't police each other or ask questions about what we do when we're not together. We have all of the fun, with none of the stupid drama that makes relationships such a pain in the ass. It's perfect."

"How would that change if he came to a meeting?" Gina asks.

"First he comes to a meeting, next he's telling me what to wear and to make him a sandwich. Gradually it escalates until I'm checking in with him before I go to the bathroom. I don't need a damn boyfriend telling me what to do."

Gina looks closely at her dear friend. "It's not going to go like that. Not with Nick."

Brigitte is having none of it. "I already know how it goes. Brigitte gets lost and it becomes all about 'we.' 'We hated that movie.' 'We plan to buy a house in the suburbs.' 'We decided that Brigitte's soul was superfluous so we sold it and used the money to expand Nick's Dictators of the World action figure collection.' Fuck that."

"But Nick seems to value his freedom and independence as much as you value yours," Gina says.

"He says he does, but I've heard that song before. As soon as a man gets his claws into you, it starts. He wants to change you, tone you down, shape you into the image of his ideal."

Gina says, "It doesn't always happen. Lawrence lets me be myself."

Brigitte ripostes, "See? He 'lets' you. That's exactly the trap I want to avoid."

"It's not like that. He appreciates who I am. I don't feel trapped at all. I love Lawrence."

"And I love Nick. I just prefer to love him at a distance. I love giraffes too, but I wouldn't want one following me around everywhere I go."

They arrive at the community center. Despite the eye-watering cheese fragrance, the place is packed. After a few preliminaries and pleasantries, the women get down to the businesses at hand: knitting and stopping rape. Christine continues with her lovely socks, Suzie struggles with her boa with sparkles, and Jasmine works on a pair of knitted gloves to wear instead of her mittens. The women begin talking.

"So have we seen a decrease yet in rates of rape?" Gina asks.

Suzie begins, "I've printed out some reports . . ."

At that moment Marilyn pushes her way into the crowded room. Gina clears her throat to alert Suzie, and Jasmine blurts, "Incoming!"

Suzie spots Marilyn and attempts a save, "Um, reports from the American Knitting Association on dwindling surplus yarn supplies . . ."

Marilyn says, "Mom. We need to talk."

Gina says, "Oh, Marilyn! I'm so glad to see you! We were just talking about the latest knitting research. It's fascinating. And so important, now that knitting's bursting in popularity."

Marilyn says, "I know what you're doing."

"Making absolutely gorgeous sweaters?"

"How could you?"

"Talent and creativity?"

"How could you respond to violence with more violence?"

Gina says, "It's not the same."

But Marilyn says, "It is! You're operating on their level! You're becoming just like they are!"

Brigitte snorts, and Gina shoots her a look.

Gina says, "No, Marilyn, my darling. I've never raped anyone. A woman who kills a rapist—not that anyone here has ever done such a thing—does not become a rapist."

Everyone can see Marilyn's next statement coming.

"Violence is wrong."

Gina responds, sensibly, "I agree. And that's why we're putting a stop to it. Permanently."

Soon after, Marilyn storms into her house, slams the door and calls out, "Dad? Dad!"

He responds from the living room, "Hi, honey!"

"Dad. You have to do something about Mom. It was bad enough when we thought she was a poet. Now she's a murderer!"

Lawrence becomes stern. "Marilyn, don't say that about your mother. She has never been a poet. And 'murderer'—I don't know if that's exactly the word I would use. That seems a little harsh to me."

Marilyn is nearly in tears. She says, "What if everybody finds out? How will I hold my head up in school? My mother, the murderer. I get good grades. I show school spirit. I'm in the marching band. And now Mom has wrecked it all by becoming a serial killer! How could she do this to me?"

"Wellll . . ."

"She's so selfish. She's ruining my life!"

Having bought time with several Ls and some ellipses, Lawrence has an answer.

"Selfish? Marilyn, do you really think she's doing this for herself?" He pauses, then says, "She's doing this for you."

"For me? But I don't want her to do it!"

He asks, "Have you ever walked alone down a dark street and heard footfalls behind you?"

"Yeah, but—"

"Were you afraid?"

"Yeah, so?"

"Have you ever been alone in a subway car late at night and had a strange man sit too close, and look at you in a way you don't like?"

Marilyn says, lower lip pouting, "Your point is?"

"Did that scare you?"

"Yes, but—"

Lawrence continues, "Did a boy ever say he'd drive you home from school, and you refused because you weren't sure he wouldn't take you someplace else?"

Marilyn's face closes off. She says, "I don't want to talk about it."

Lawrence concludes, "That is why your mother is doing this. She's doing it for you, so you don't have to be afraid."

Marilyn sputters, "Oh, Daddy, I hate it when you do that!"

"Do what, darling?"

"When you talk sense to me like that! It makes me so mad." She glares at him.

Lawrence thinks a moment, then says, "Well, if you want to talk to someone who won't talk sense to you, maybe you should go talk to—"

"Yes! I knew I should have gone to Brigitte in the first place. I'll go see her tomorrow. Parents never understand anything."

It is a bright early afternoon. Marilyn strides up Brigitte's walk and knocks on her door. She hears strains of Bollywood music coming from inside. No answer. She knocks louder. No answer. She pounds on the door, hard. She shouts, "Brigitte! Brigitte! Open up!"

The door opens. Loud music pours into the street. Brigitte peers out. She's wearing a sparkly belly dancer's outfit.

"Marilyn, what a pleasant surprise! You can join me in the

dance! Come on girl, let's recalibrate our chakras with a little booty-shaking magic!" Brigitte starts belly dancing and takes Marilyn's hands, pulling her inside.

Marilyn is reluctant and annoyed. She pulls her hands away. She shouts over the music, "I didn't come to dance. I came to talk to you."

Brigitte responds, "Vigorous dancing makes any problem more manageable. I've read studies."

"Not. In. The. Mood."

"Oh, good. Grumpiness helps a lot."

Marilyn says, "See? This is exactly the problem. You don't take things seriously enough. You're frivolous."

Brigitte smiles ingenuously. "Thank you."

Marilyn insists, "It's not a compliment!" She looks past Brigitte and notices that the television is on, and the music comes not from a CD, but a DVD. She notices that the people singing are wearing green uniforms and carrying guns. She says, in that tone of voice with which anyone who knows a teenager is so familiar, "What the hell?"

"What? This is a movie about the indigenous Naxalite rebellion in India. What's wrong with that?"

"But . . . they're singing."

"And revolutionaries aren't supposed to sing and dance and make love? A revolution without songs is like a catfish without whiskers. It's like a great grandmother without liver spots. It's like an egg without a yolk. It's like cheese without . . ."

"I get it! Stop!"

"Just because George Washington's dentures didn't fit, we think revolutionaries are supposed to be sourpussed old farts. But revolution can be fun, and I've got the DVDs and CDs to prove it!"

Marilyn tries to interject, "Brigitte!"

Brigitte turns off the TV, then dashes to her CD holder. She says, "Would you like to hear *Show Tunes of the Wobblies*? No? How about *Love Ballads of the Spanish Anarchists*? Still no? Maybe *The Tibetan Armed Resistance Movement Sings Show Tunes from Hello Dalai*? How about, *Just Say No to Opium and to the Running Dogs of Capitalism and Empire*, by The Boxer Rebellion Boys? *Mend Your Heart and Mend the Land (and Kick Out the Fucking Oil Companies)*, by The Movement for the Emancipation of the Niger Delta Full Men's and Women's Choir? No?"

Brigitte suddenly stops. The room is silent. Finally she says, "Call me psychic. I sense that something is bothering you. I'll get some tea."

Marilyn: "No tea."

"Coffee?"

"No coffee."

"Cola? Juice? Cocktail? Water? Herbal infusion? Milk?"

"I'm not thirsty!" Marilyn cries. "I have an issue here! I'm trying to talk to you!"

Brigitte sits, folds her hands on her lap, and says, "I'm listening."

"Finally!" Marilyn says. "I'm worried about what you're doing with the knitting circle. You're putting my mom in danger."

Brigitte shakes her head, says, "I'm not doing any such thing. We're eliminating danger."

Marilyn throws up her hands in an exasperated flounce: "You're killing people! My mother would never do that on her own."

Brigitte is matter-of-fact: "It's an activity best done as a group."

Marilyn stares, says, "You're a bad influence."

Brigitte says, calmly, "That's untrue. If anything, it's the other way around."

"What? How so?"

"Well," Brigitte answers. "I'm a go-getter. I get things done. I get bad things gone. Your mother is, shall we say, not as proactive. I won't say stuffy. I won't say stodgy. I won't say blah. She is my best friend, after all. But if anyone's a bad influence, a drag on the fun and rambunctiousness of our little group, it's certainly not me."

Marilyn puts her hands on her hips. She says, "Listen. I understand that rapists are bad people and we don't want them walking among us, menacing everyone—"

Brigitte interjects, "Women."

"What?"

"Menacing women. Some men, but primarily women."

"Menacing women they come in contact with. But violence is wrong."

Brigitte answers calmly, "The violence they perpetrate—"

Marilyn waves her off. "I know what you're going to say. Allowing them to be violent and not stopping them is the moral equivalent of being violent yourself."

Brigitte claps her hands once, not patronizingly at all, stands up, and says, "Precisely. You get it! Are we done?"

"No!" Marilyn takes a deep breath, then continues, "I'm not saying you should just let rapists run around loose. I'm saying that vigilantism is bad for society. You can't just take the law into your own hands."

Brigitte raises her eyebrows. "In whose hands would it be more effective? Cops and the court system? I couldn't possibly do a worse job wielding the law than they do."

"But where does it end? Can just anyone decide what is a crime and what isn't? Or who should be punished and who shouldn't? You're asking for social chaos."

"Marilyn, social chaos is when 25 percent of all women are raped and another 19 percent have to fend off rapes, and nothing is done about it. I don't think it's so hard to figure out that stopping rapists is going to solve that problem."

Marilyn cries, "But the knitting circle women can't wantonly kill people!"

For the first time Brigitte's voice becomes the tiniest bit sharp, as she says, "Wanton? Who said anything about wanton?" She strides toward a huge book, open on a small desk.

Marilyn whines, "Not the dictionary!"

Brigitte looks at her. "Young lady! How will you ever advance in life without an estimable vocabulary?" Brigitte searches the dictionary, finds what she's looking for, and reads, "wanton: lacking in moral restraint." Brigitte smiles, then says, more or less to herself, "What *do* they teach young people in school these days?"

Marilyn frowns.

Brigitte continues, "I think we're showing great restraint. We're only going after rapists so far."

Marilyn's eyes go wide. She gasps, "So far?"

Brigitte says, "Of course. What about pornographers? What about Hollywood filmmakers who show a man forcing himself on a woman, and at the beginning of the scene she's pushing him away, but by the end she's wrapping her arms around him and pulling him close? And what about those awful advertisers who use our bodies to sell everything from beer to gum to automobiles? What about—"

Marilyn interrupts: "You and your knitting circle can't just kill people!"

"I think we can. We're doing a fine job, too."

"But there's already a group that's supposed to stop criminals. They're called the police."

Brigitte snorts derisively.

Marilyn continues, "Yes, the police. I'm not ashamed to say it. Why can't you let them do their jobs, instead of taking it upon yourselves to commit horrible violence?"

Brigitte once again becomes slightly sharp. "Marilyn. Do not insult our violence. It is not horrible. It's very artistic, innovative, and skilled. You think it's easy to create such masterful and righteous violence? You think the police could do that?"

"The police don't have to kill people! They could do this without violence. They could just put people in jail."

"You don't think putting people in jail is violent?"

"Of course it isn't."

"Are you saying that if the police ask nicely, rapists will peacefully stroll into jail cells and volunteer to stay there?"

"Well, no. Of course they have to be forced into the cells. And the cells have to be locked."

Brigitte asks, "In your experience, can anyone be forced to do anything without violence or the threat of violence?"

"If you make them feel bad about themselves . . ."

"If committing rape doesn't make a man feel bad about himself, I think he's a little beyond guilt-tripping, don't you?"

Marilyn thinks a moment. "Well, my mom is really good at making people feel guilty."

"True."

"But I guess even she would have a hard time with some of those guys."

Brigitte nods. "And if she can't do it, no one can."

They smile at each other.

CHAPTER 4

The police war room looks precisely like what you would expect a police war room to look like. It has wanted posters, certificates of certification, Styrofoam cups of steaming coffee, half-filled boxes of pizza, a terrarium containing a garter snake, a softball trophy, a bowling trophy, an extensive library of police procedure manuals, including *Forensics for the Overqualified*, a copy of *Les Miserables* (described as a stirring tale of the brave and tragic Lestrade who refuses to give up on the world's second most famous literary cold case; the most famous literary cold case is covered by the books: *Who Really Killed Jesus?* and, for a more academic and judicial perspective, in the *You Be the Judge* series of legal comic books, *The Execution of Jesus, Volume 1: Death Penalty Gone Wrong, or Fry the Bastard* and *The Execution of Jesus, Volume 2: Would the Supreme Court Have Overturned the Decision?*) a copy of *The Trial*, and three televisions: one tuned to ESPN, one tuned to Judge Judy, and the third showing endlessly repeating loops of Jack Bauer's greatest hits.

The chief stands at the front of the room. Cops sit in chairs, facing him. He says, "These serial killings are an embarrassment to the city and to our department. We must catch these perps as soon as possible."

One of the cops, a relentlessly ambitious, relentlessly handsome man—with a jaw of marble, steely blue eyes, coal-black hair, a hint of silver in his carefully trimmed mustache, bronzed skin, six-pack (aluminum can) abs, a rock-hard grip, a tin ear, and an ironclad alibi for anything anyone might accuse him of—is named Flint. He says, "We know these women are behind it. All we have to do is prove it."

Another cop, named Rico (a burly man, a man's man, a man so manly that each matted hair on the backs of his hands oozes tiny drops of gleaming testosterone), asks, "How do we do that?"

Flint smirks. "It's a bunch of women. How hard can it be?"

The chief makes his decision known: "We'll send in an infiltrator. It'll take about five minutes to crack this case." He looks at Flint and says, "Stone, you're volunteering."

Flint shows his pearly white teeth. "I can outsmart them, no problem. I'll take them down."

The chief hands Flint some knitting needles and yarn. "Learn how to do this."

Flint pauses, then asks, "You want me . . . to learn how to knit?"

The chief nods decisively. "Make them believe you're one of them."

"But . . . knitting?"

"You've had other tough assignments."

"C'mon, Chief. I've got a family and a reputation. Send me back undercover with the Slaughterio Crime Family drug operation. Anything but this."

"You volunteered. You're going."

Today is Swiss cheese day at the factory, and the women keep thinking of ham sandwiches.

After a spirited but inconclusive debate on the merits of yellow mustard versus Dijon, Brigitte asks, "Do you have the list of rapists we need to neutralize this week?"

Suzie holds up a piece of paper. She says, "I was thinking

Jasmine and I could handle A through F. Mary and Christine could take G through L."

Flint walks into the room and sits down. He starts knitting, slowly. His tongue protrudes in concentration. The women silently watch him. He continues knitting for a painfully long time. No one says a word.

Brigitte catches Gina's eye, motions her into a back room. Once out of hearing, Brigitte whispers, "Something about him isn't right."

Gina nods vigorously, and whispers back, "I know! Did you notice how he always drops his last stitch?"

Brigitte says, "We need to get rid of him."

"But how?"

"Leave it to me."

The two return to the main room and sit down.

Brigitte asks the group, "So, has anyone seen that new shade of Revlon, Siren's Kiss?"

Jasmine catches on immediately. She squeals, "Oh. My. God! It's divine! I was thinking of wearing it with Go to Bed Red polish on my fingernails, and Mad Lust on my toenails, which matches perfectly with these new strappy stilettos I got at the mall. Remember, Suzie? The ones I showed you?"

Suzie squeals back, "Per!Fect! I love those shoes!" She gushes to the group, "They have really thin straps around the ankle, like a quarter-inch wide . . . no, like an eighth of an inch. Maybe a quarter. Jaz, was it a quarter or an eighth?"

Jasmine says enthusiastically, "More like an eighth. They're, like, thin and delicate and they cross twice over the foot before going up like this." She pantomimes the straps going up her ankle.

Christine says, "They sound darling! And they remind me

of some shoes my granddaughter wanted me to buy her for her birthday. Can you imagine such a little girl wanting heels?"

Flint sighs, packs up his knitting, and starts to leave.

Mary says to him, "Oh, dearie, where are you going? The fun has barely even started."

Flint replies, "That's what I was afraid of."

The police are meeting again in the war room. While they wait for Flint, the chief refreshes himself on techniques of detection by reading *The Collected Works of Edgar Allen Poe.* He stops, underlines a phrase, then looks up at Rico and says thoughtfully, "I just had an idea. Is it possible that the killer could be an Orang-Outang?"

Before Rico can answer, in walks Flint.

The chief says, "And?"

Flint says, "I can't take it, Chief. They're brutal, monstrous."

The chief says, "Brutal, eh? Like an Orang-Outang?"

Flint replies, "Worse, boss. Worse than you can imagine."

The chief dismisses Flint with a small gesture, then turns to Rico, says, "You're in. Let's see if you can fight some crime without sniveling like a little girl."

As the police file out of the room, they hear the chief give Rico one last piece of advice: "Make sure not to let them make a monkey out of you."

It's cream cheese week, and the day is so hot you could use the sidewalk to fry bacon. It's Thursday, and the Knitting Circle is meeting.

In walks someone who looks like a man, a burly man, a manly man oozing testosterone from the matted hairs on the backs of his hands. His low V-necked sweater reveals what would normally be a décolletage, only with hair. Lots of it, as thick and matted as a 1970s shag carpet on which decades of beers have spilled and been left to dry into a yeasty crust. Beneath the sweater he wears a bra that is clearly full of something besides human flesh. And below his waist he wears a tastefully short plaid skirt that shows off his muscular, hairy legs. He is carrying a new copy of Camille Paglia's *Sexual Personae*. He sits down.

The women of the Knitting Circle look at him.

The man says, "Ahem."

The women knit.

The man says, "My name is Ric . . . Ric . . . Raquel, and I'm here to do some serious knittin'."

The women knit.

Rico continues, "I've had it up to my tight sweet round ass with the Man, with Patriarchy. You know what I'm sayin', girlfriends?"

The women knit.

Rico continues, "I'm tired of men gropin' me, tired of them lookin' at me with their x-ray eyes, tired of them seein' my secret treasures."

The women knit.

Rico continues, "And I'm tired of stayin' home, slavin' all day at cookin' and cleanin', and then watchin' soap operas and Oprah and Dr. Phil and Judge Judy, while my man sweats away his life to bring home a paycheck. And I'm tired of that filthy beastly man with eight hands wantin' a piece of me."

The women knit.

Rico notes, "He's hung like a horse, by the way."

Brigitte stifles a laugh.

Rico says, "I'm just sayin'."

The women knit.

Rico says, "And I'm tired of goin' through a divorce where the lousy biased judge only gives me half of the house that my ex-husband worked his fingers to the bone for, and I'm tired of takin' only 50 percent of his salary for the rest of his miserable life as he continues to put his self on the line to keep the streets safe for all of us."

The women stop knitting, stare at Rico for a moment, then resume knitting.

Rico says, "I'm ready to bring down the whole patriarchy. Let's do some serious ass-kickin', bra-burnin' knittin'!"

The women knit.

Rico is by the moment becoming more comfortable in his role, and more excited. He moves toward crescendo: "And I know where there are some rapos ripe for some serious knittin', if you get my drift. Who's with me? Yee-haw! Let's do it!"

The women knit.

Rico whoops, "Rock and Roll!"

Suzie asks, casually, "Jasmine, how did those shoes look with that lipstick you got yesterday?"

Jasmine responds, "Ohmygod, ohmygod, Oh my god! They looked so hot! I wore them to Club Xanadu. You know the one?"

Suzie says, "Oh, the Xan? The club with the lights? And the music?"

"You know the place!"

"Girlygirlygirl, who doesn't?"

Jasmine, "And I met this really cute guy!"

Mary asks, "What does he do for a living?"

"He said he sells stocks and bonds, or maybe he's a bail bondsman or something like that. You know, high finance. Oh, he mentioned selling blood. That's it!"

Mary nods. "That's nice—he has a steady job."

Jasmine says, "But the best part is, he has this gorgeous smile."

Christine asks, "Good teeth?"

Rico's eyes flutter, and he seems to be having a hard time breathing.

Jasmine says, "Great teeth! And he totally loved my shoes!"

"Totally?" Suzie squeals.

"Totally. I could tell. And he said I was foxy. Except he said it like, 'fox-ay.'"

"Fox-ay."

Rico pulls a tissue from his bra to wipe his sweaty forehead.

Jasmine effuses, "He called me Foxy Lady."

Suzie follows up, "Only he said it 'fox-ay'?"

"Yes, he said it was from an old song by Hendrix."

Suzie says, "I *love* Johnny Hendrix!"

Rico's eyes flutter again. He can barely vocalize, "It's Jimi."

Suzie barely looks at him, says, "Jimi, Johnny. Whatev. The important thing is he said she was fox-ay."

Christine adds, "And that he had good teeth."

Suzie continues, "And that he loved her shoes."

Gina asks, "Were they the ones with the really thin straps?"

Jasmine squeals again, says, "Yes, like a quarter inch. Or maybe it's an eighth. Suze?"

Suzie answers, "Definitely an eighth."

Rico's eyelids flutter, his eyes roll back in his head, and then he falls out of his chair and onto the floor, insensate.

The police are in their war room. This time the chief is reading Agatha Christie. He stops reading, ponders, then says, "Do you think the rapists are killing each other one by one, and when there are only two left each will think the other is the murderer, so one rapist will kill the other, and then out of guilt and remorse hang himself? But then we will all discover that the real murderer was one of the earlier victims, who only faked his death. Yes, I think that's right. Pretty damned ingenious of me to figure this out, I'd say. So, to solve the crime we only need discover which of the victims is not actually dead. Flint, can you handle that?"

Flint responds, "Um, sir, all of the victims are dead."

"Dead?"

"As dinosaurs, sir."

"Someone told me that dinosaurs evolved into chickens, so they're really not dead. Maybe we should look into that."

"Look into chickens, sir?"

"No, the victims!"

"But the victims are all dead."

"Really? That's damned inconvenient of them. Damn it all to hell. How will we solve the case if all the murder victims are actually dead?"

"I'm not sure, sir."

An officer named Sandy Dougher sits in the back of the room. She is beautiful. As beautiful as the Mona Lisa. As beautiful as the sweeping boughs of a western red cedar. As beautiful as the delicate scent of frangipani on a cool breeze on a tropical evening. As beautiful as a ringing line drive into the gap in left-center field. As beautiful as a sharp kick to a rapist's testicles.

She sits near Lieutenant Chuck Kort. Some might think she detests him. Maybe it's the daggered looks she gives him. Maybe it's the way she otherwise will not look him in the face. Maybe it's the way when not required to remain she leaves the room when he enters. Maybe it's the telephone number block she's installed on her landline. Maybe it's the ID checkpoints her neighborhood watch helped her install to keep him away. Maybe it's the pictures of Chuck Kort displayed prominently in the machine-gun turret her landlord helped her install on the corner of the apartment building.

The chief says, "We're doing something wrong. What could it be?"

Sandy says, "Uh, Chief?"

The chief speaks over her, "What should we do?"

She answers, "What if we do our jobs and stop rapists?"

The chief looks around the room, waiting for someone to respond to his question.

Sandy says again, "What if we do our jobs and stop rapists?"

The chief continues to look around the room, still waiting for someone to respond to his question.

Chuck turns to Sandy and says, "If women don't want it, why do they dress the way they do?"

Sandy scowls in his general direction.

Chuck continues, softly enough so only Sandy can hear, "Why do they parade around with hips and breasts, huh? Your body tells me you want it. You can say no, but your body always begs for it."

Sandy's scowl turns even fiercer as she curls her body, which happens to be fully covered by her uniform, away from Chuck. "Don't talk to me," she hisses.

Chuck says, "You know you loved it."

The chief says, "You in back, shh. We're trying to figure out what to do about these knitting needle murderers. They've got our balls in a wringer, all right."

Sandy says to the chief, "I have an idea."

The chief says, "I wish someone had an idea."

Sandy says, "I'll go in, Chief."

The chief says, "I know it's a rough assignment, but doesn't even one of you who have the balls to act like a woman? Won't any of you volunteer?"

Sandy raises her hand. "I volunteer. I was the Regional Knitting Champion in high school, and later I won the Golden Needle, the Pulitzer Prize of the Fiber Arts world. I can fit in with them, no problem."

The chief says, "It's going to cost so much to train one of you to knit. Don't any of you already know how?"

Another cop speaks up, "I saw Sandy knitting in the break room. Why don't we send her?"

The chief says, "That's a brilliant idea. I'll remember that when you're next up for promotion."

This week the cheese is Ossau-Iraty, a rare cheese made only from the milk of black-faced Manech sheep, a cheese known for its luscious ivory color and its slightly acidic slightly hazelnut taste. As the women begin knitting, they are overcome by emotion at the beauty of the smell. Some close their eyes. Some stare into space. Some weep silently.

Sandy Dougher walks in. She sits down.

The knitters leave their reverie, slowly, regretfully, as if waking from a wondrous dream they know they will soon forget.

Sandy says to them, "I know you're not stupid. I'm a cop. I've been sent here to shut you down, but I'm really here for other reasons."

Gina shakes her head slightly, to bring herself fully awake. Then she says to the group, "Today we are going to learn some of the Fair Isle knitting techniques."

Sandy continues, "I also know you can't trust a cop unless you have good reason. Please just watch the news tomorrow." She rises to leave and hands Gina a slip of paper. She says, "Listen for this name."

Gina reads the name aloud to the group, "'Lieutenant Chuck Kort.'" She turns to Sandy, says, "Who's this?"

Sandy responds, "Let's just say he fits the profile."

The next evening, the television is on again. Franz Maihem no longer looks like Jesus, but more like Jeremiah, with overtones of Howard Beale, Lonesome Rhodes, Jimmy Swaggart, and an elderly Bela Lugosi, as depicted by Jimmy Stewart circa 1956. He stares into the camera, into the very souls of his flock, and says, mournfully, "Tragedy struck again this morning for our heroic men in blue. Lieutenant Chuck Kort was found in the precinct break room, pinned to a vending machine with a knitting needle to the throat. If these terrorists can strike in the hallowed halls of a police station, they can strike anywhere. Be afraid. Be very afraid."

We are back in the war room. The chief is now reading *The Complete Adventures of Sherlock Holmes*. He stops, looks around the room, and asks piercingly, "What do you hear?"

No one says anything for a moment, till Flint says, "Nothing, Chief."

The chief looks at them, triumphant, and exclaims, "Exactly! And that is the clue we've been waiting for." When no one responds, his look becomes as piercing as was his voice. He takes in each person, one by one. They are all wearing black armbands with their uniforms, except for Sandy, who is wearing bright pink. He says to her, "You are not showing proper respect for our fallen brother."

She responds, "I have to wear this—I'm undercover. Don't worry; my underwear is black."

Flint perks up, says, "And lacy?"

The chief says to her, "I hope you have some good news for us. We need to catch these lunatics. Sure, if they kill rapists, we'll do our duty and investigate, whatever. But these fiends have attacked two of our own, one right here in our fortress! This means war. Have you found anything?"

"I've been to several meetings now, and I think we're on to something. This group is hot."

"How hot?"

"Very hot."

"Give us the full report, then."

"The full report?"

"They're hot?"

"Very hot."

"Full report."

Sandy takes a deep breath before she begins, "So, Jasmine recently purchased a pair of stilettos. . . ."

The chief interrupts, "Stilettos. That's definitely an escalation over knitting needles."

Sandy continues, "Stiletto shoes with skinny straps, that are either a quarter or an eighth of an inch. . . ."

Flint says, "Here it comes."

Rico blurts, "Please, God. No."

The chief asks, "Can you get to the point?"

Sandy says, "I told you they were hot. And I think I can get them to give me some information."

The chief urges her to continue.

She says, "Well, Jasmine is thinking of changing her nail

polish from Go to Bed Red to Hot Slut, and we're all wondering whether her new boyfriend, well, we're not sure if he's actually her new boyfriend, since he hasn't actually called her, will like the new shade better than the old."

Rico begs, "Chief, make her stop."

But Sandy talks over him: "I haven't gotten to the good part yet. Suzie needs a major change in her life, and she's wondering whether bangs would be sufficient . . ."

The chief asks, "Bangs, as in explosives?"

Sandy continues, "Or whether she'll need to go all the way."

The chief leans forward. "'All the way' as in, come clean and become an informant? Or, accelerate the murders?"

Sandy answers, "'All the way' as in change her hair color."

Rico wails, "I can't take it."

Sandy keeps going, "And if she does, should she whisper with shimmering gold highlights, or shout with a shocking bright red-orange or a dramatic sable-black?"

Rico sways in his chair.

Sandy says, "And after that, is she going to want to go with an Aveda Black Malva Color Conditioner, or more of a Pantene Pro-V Brunette Expressions Daily Color Enhancing Shampoo?"

Rico clutches his heart, starts to fall from his chair. His last words before hitting the floor are, "Mother of Mercy, is this the end of Rico?"

CHAPTER 5

Five men sit on mismatched thrift-store sofas in a room lit by four weak and failing light bulbs set in three different yet equally hideous lamp fixtures. One fixture is composed of taxidermied squirrel frozen in the act of scratching a ceramic pine stump, with a shade crafted of old neckties. Another is a plastic monkey wearing a vest and holding a light bulb in each hand. A third has a red pump shoe for a base, and a fishnet stocking–clad female mannequin leg for a post. The bare bulb sticks out at a fifteen-degree angle at the top.

The room is carpeted in cruddy red shag, with walls lined with peeling fake wood paneling. Crucifixes compete with praying hands for wall space around a poster of Jesus wearing camo fatigues and pointing at the viewer, with the caption, "Jesus wants YOU to save some souls." A fiberboard bookshelf held together with duct tape stands in one corner. Nestled within are seven stolen Gideon Bibles, the complete *Left Behind* series, a clearly-intentionally-mangled sacrificial copy of *Harry Potter and the Sorcerer's Stone*, a DVD of *Cats*, a CD of *Ted Nugent Plays Gospel Favorites*, and an ancient and well-read copy of *Everything You Always Wanted to Know about Sex, But Were Afraid to Ask*, all book-ended by a pair of carved wooden NASCAR Jesuses.

The men wear baby blue T-shirts with the letters MAWAR stenciled beneath an awkwardly designed logo: the circle/arrow symbol for "male" surrounding a clenched fist with a cross sprouting from the second knuckle like an upraised middle finger.

The first man, clearly the leader, says, "The cops still hath their heads up their asses, fuckin' wankers."

The rest of the group responds with a hearty "Amen!"

The first man continues, "These pussies hath not the balls to even catch a bunch of dumb females. We hath to perform their job for them while they waveth around their dicks."

The group responds, "Praise the Lord!"

One of the MAWAR members, Billy Bob, asks another, "Brother Zebadiah, hast thou initiated the holy plan to grab that heathen ditz Jasmine?"

Zebadiah responds, "I have, Brother Billy Bob. I have seen the infidel many times at a pernicious den of sin called Xanadu. I have seen her even this last night. And I have called her by the name of 'Fox-ay.' Having seen this woman many times, I feel she is now in the palm of my hand, ready to feel the mighty fury of the *Lord*."

Billy Bob nods. "Brother, you got you some holy fuckin' nads of steel to come in such close proximity to such a Jezebel. What comes next?"

Zebadiah answers, "Phase Two of our holy plan begins in three days."

"Praise Jesus. But why not tomorrow?"

"It's the three-day rule. If you call one of these wanton hussies before three days, she turns down even the Holiest of Holy men. If you wait three days, she's yours."

It is late at night. Marilyn sits alone in her family's dark living room. The front door opens. "Mom?" Marilyn calls.

Gina enters and asks, "What are you doing up so late?"

"What are you doing *out* so late? It's 2 a.m.!"

"I outgrew my curfew a few years ago. I get to stay out as

late as I want. When you're a mother, you'll get to do the same thing."

Marilyn says, with only a half-hearted sneer, "I hate it when you use that tone."

Gina responds, "When you're a mother you'll get to use this tone, too."

Marilyn's sneer is gone entirely. She says, sincerely, "It's just I worry about you getting into trouble."

Gina hugs Marilyn. "I know what I'm doing, kiddo."

"You wouldn't let me get by with that," Marilyn says.

Gina says, predictably, "When you're a mother . . ."

Marilyn hesitates, then begins, "I guess the reason I stayed up is that I wanted to tell you that I understand what you're doing. I understand now why you're doing it. And it's . . . it's okay."

Gina hugs her again, and says, "That means an awful lot to me. Thank you, Marilyn."

"But I still can't go along with it. I can't join you," Marilyn says.

Gina responds, "That's okay, honey. I would never ask you to go against your principles."

A comfortable silence passes between them. Then Gina pulls a pair of knitting needles from her purse. "I want to ask you, though, to carry these. You don't have to use them. Just keep them handy. In case you ever need them." She holds them out, waiting.

Marilyn hesitates, and then takes them.

A few days later, Jasmine and Suzie sit inside the Red Moon Sacred Gyn Mill Tea House for Wimmin of All Kinds and Kindreds. Several signs on the walls make clear that this tea house "does not discriminate on the basis of gender, sexual preference, race, skin color, skin tone, the relative smoothness and softness of one's skin, nationality of origin, religious preference, height, weight, age, food preferences, driving record, species, handedness, competence at chess, literacy, hair color, hair length, soap choices, food allergies, chemical sensitivities, fatigue, neuroses, phobias, past lives, astrological signs, clothing, boots, pocket-knife preference, brand of pickup, or canine/feline/companion animal preference. Nor does it descriminate on the basis of misspellings or typos."

Another sign states, "If you mention calories, you WILL be asked to leave." By the silverware a sign reads, "Sisters: we refrain from the patriarchal weapons of knives and forks when nurturing ourselves and each other. Please use the healing womb of a spoon." Yet another sign comforts customers: "13 hugs are healing." The teahouse's slogan is painted on the wall behind the cash register: "Where there's not a single penis between us."

The saltshaker is inscribed with the words, "The Gift of Mother Ocean." Exposed wood beams on the ceiling read, "The Gift of Mother Forest." A ceramic vase on the table is inscribed, "The Gift of Mother Earth." The tampon dispenser in the bathroom is inscribed, "The Gift of Mother Moon."

The handmade mugs have ceramic breasts. The plates are shaped like 3D vulvas, providing a convenient crevice in which to rest the spoons. Customers intent on consuming every crumb of dessert are often driven to probe the plates' folds with determined tongues.

Jasmine and Suzie are looking at the menu, trying to decide between: 1) wheat-free, dairy-free, sugar-free carob pie sweetened with lemon juice; 2) wheat-free, dairy-free, sugar-free gingerbread wimmin and gyrl cookies, anatomically correct;

3) wheat-free, dairy-free, sugar-free cookies with oregano/basil flour; 4) a wheat-free, dairy-free, sugar-free ice creme sundae; 5) wheat-free, dairy-free, sugar-free, caffeine-free brownies; and 6) triple chocolate cheesecake called "Praise the Lourde!"

It does not take them long to choose number six. Once they are seated, Jasmine can no longer contain her excitement. She blurts, "He asked me out!"

"Finally! Congratulations! Where?" Suzie asks.

"I don't know yet. I have to call him. Do you think I should call right away, or wait until tomorrow? I should keep him waiting, right? Be friendly but not too-too available, right?"

Suzie doesn't focus on the question, but on Jaz's first sentence. "What do you mean you don't know where? What did he say?"

Jasmine holds up her cell phone so Suzie can see a text message.

Suzie reads, "'U R hot. Can I C U?' Jaz. That's his invitation? . . . Um . . . " Jasmine begins to look worried, so Suzie switches tone and gushes, "Wow! He asked you out!"

Jasmine responds, "Suzie, I know it might be too soon to say this, but I think he might be The One!"

Gina and Lawrence are lying in their sensible bed. A fair while ago they made some very sensible love—and Gina was neither stuffy nor stodgy nor blah, and she was indeed proactive; beyond that we will leave Gina's and Lawrence's sexual activities to Gina and Lawrence—and after caressing and chatting and snuggling and generally lingering, they—and this part is not nearly so sensible—turn on the television.

They see Franz Maihem.

Lawrence asks, "Doesn't he remind you of someone?"

Gina looks closely. "He reminds me of . . . No, I don't see it. Who does he remind you of?"

Lawrence says, "Well . . . I guess he doesn't remind me of . . . No! Wait! I've got it. He reminds me of Howdy Doody!"

"Yes! Except without the red hair!"

"And without the freckles!"

"And not so cute!"

"And," Lawrence adds, "You can see his strings ever so much better."

Franz is speaking with the urgency he reserves for only the most important news, like celebrity break-ups, environmental catastrophes, six-car pileups, and the latest winners of *American Idol*: "The FBI has released a shocking new profile of the knitting needle serial killers. Folks, brace yourselves. The FBI now believes that these vicious serial killers are chicks, I mean women. Yes, women. This is very shocking and bizarre because as we all know, almost all serial killers are men. To think that women would do this is extremely upsetting for everyone. After this report we'll be giving information about instant computer-assisted counseling you can access to deal with the trauma of this information. But right now, here's an urgent update from FBI profiler Chet Stirling."

Gina and Lawrence exchange a satisfied, amused look. Gina says, "Finally, they noticed."

Franz asks, "What made you realize that the killers are chicks, I mean women?"

Chet speaks with the certainty of the perpetually clueless. "Well, Franz, they're just like every normal rational serial killer in every way, but for one bizarre, freaky exception."

"What is that, Chet?"

"It's almost unheard of in the long, illustrious history and tradition of serial killing. It's fra~

"Tell us, Chet."

"All the victims are men.'

Franz cannot contain

god, Chet. That's impossib]

here for the Balzac Massa

Dismemberment Murders of ᴜ͜͡,

the creeps."

"Yes, Franz. I think that's a perfectly normal respon͜͡.

"What more can you tell us, Chet?"

Chet speaks now with the placid certainty of one who wears denial like a neatly knitted afghan comforter. "We have redubbed them the 'Ice Queen Killers.' It has a better ring to it than 'Knitting Needle Killers,' don't you think? Ice Queen Killers. Scary! Our investigations are continuing. In the meantime, we implore the public to be vigilant and to report any suspicious activity." He removes his glasses, stares straight into the camera. "To all you men out there, if your wife or girlfriend turns you down for sex too many times, we want to hear about it. If a girl won't go to the prom with you, we want to hear about it. If some beeyotch talks trash to you and disrespects you, you need to alert us immediately."

Gina and Lawrence exchange a horrified look. Gina says, "Report suspicious activity?"

Franz continues, "You heard it, folks. We have additional confirmation from an important unidentified high-level official that the killers are 'man-hating bitches.' This urgent situation will require extreme vigilance from all of us, and prompt reporting of any instance of man-hating. Hey, Katherine, you listening? Tonight, baby—you can't turn me down. Heh heh." He catches himself, pauses, then says, "I will be providing instant, up-to-

ond reports throughout the day on developments
ase. Check out my constant stream of reportage on
ok, Twitter, and Blabber."

Gina rolls on top of Lawrence, kissing and hugging him.
he says, "Watch out, I'm a terrifying man-hater!"

Lawrence calls out, "Help, help! FBI!"

They laugh and kiss.

Then Lawrence, always sensible, says, "Seriously, this raises
the stakes. I want you to be careful."

Gina considers, then answers even more sensibly, "The
only stakes that matter to me are the ones going through the
hearts of rapists."

Tolstoy famously remarked that all happy families are alike,
but every unhappy family is unhappy in its own way. That may
or may not be true, but what is certain is that it doesn't really
apply to high schools. Protestations of crazed commencement
speakers telling people that someday they'll look back on their
high school years as the happiest of their lives aside, a lot of
people in high school aren't all that happy. Yet in many ways
nearly all high schools are alike. Picture a high school hallway.
Picture the tile floor. Hear the sound of tennis shoes squeaking
on the tile. The ceiling is probably white, lit by fluorescent bulbs.
The walls hold banks of lockers painted in one of the school's
colors. Above the lockers the paint is white.

Picture this scene after a school's final bell has rung, as
students flee this prison where they are supposedly spending the
best years of their lives. As the minutes tick by there are fewer
and fewer students in the hallway.

At last there are two, and one of them is leaving.

Marilyn waves and calls to her friend, "I love what you're

doing with the yearbook theme, Chrissy!"

"Thanks! See you tomorrow," Chrissy says, and walks out the door.

Now the school is silent. Marilyn enters a girls' bathroom, goes into a stall, hangs her knapsack on a hook, crouches precariously over the bowl without touching anything (well-trained daughter of a sensible germ-phobic mother), and pees, humming the Naxalite Rebellion Bollywood theme song she frustratingly hasn't been able to get out of her head. She flushes, takes down her knapsack, and opens the stall door.

An older boy is standing inches in front of her, one hand on each side of the stall's doorway.

Marilyn gasps. "Jason! You can't be in here!"

"I am though, aren't I? And so are you," he says.

She asks, "What do you want, the history assignment?"

"I want something else."

He's way too close. She laughs nervously. He takes a lock of her hair between his fingers, tugs on it, and glares at her. Marilyn is confused and a little scared.

She says, "What's up with you?"

He doesn't respond. She pushes between his body and the opening of the stall, then tries to reach the door. He grabs her arm and pushes her backward against a counter. Her knapsack drops into a sink. He grinds his hips into hers. She tries to push him away, but he's stronger.

She says, "What the fuck are you doing?"

"You said *no* the other night when I drove you home, but you're not going to say *no* now."

"Get off me!"

He whines, "When you rejected me, you broke my heart."

Marilyn tries to placate him. "I didn't reject *you*, Jason; I like you fine. I just didn't want to, you know . . ."

"Why not? What's wrong with me, huh?" He squeezes her breasts and forces a kiss.

She turns her face away, says, "Stop it!"

He says, "I've got what you need, Marilyn. Trust me, you'll enjoy it. It'll be *so* good. Feel this, this is how much I want you." He puts her hand on his crotch.

She snatches her hand away, horrified. "Stop it! *No!*"

"Shhh," he says, quietly. "Shhh. We're made for each other. You'll see. Just surrender to our love."

Marilyn struggles as Jason kisses her face and neck, as he rubs his body against hers, as he touches her body with his hands. Unable to free herself, she begins to cry.

Marilyn shouts, "Help! Help! Someone!"

Jason's not worried. He informs her, "Everyone's gone home. Yell all you want. Soon you'll be yelling for more."

Marilyn begins to sob. She says, "Never! No! Stop! Jason, you can't do this!"

"Oh, yes, I can." He tears open Marilyn's shirt and pushes up her bra. She tries to pull his hands off her, and fails. She says, frantic, "Jason, think about what you're doing! You're going too far! You're supposed to be my friend!"

"I *am* your friend. We're much more than friends. I want you and I'm going to have you. I'm going to fuck you so hard. I love you so much."

"If you love me you'll stop! You'll listen to me! Please stop this—we can work it out! No one has to know about this! Please!"

He says, "Hush now. You had your chance to do this nice." With one hand Jason reaches behind her, pulls her close, crushing her against him. With his other hand he pulls up her skirt.

"I understand I made you feel bad when I wouldn't do what you wanted, and I'm sorry, I'm so sorry! I didn't mean to hurt your feelings! Let's talk about this, Jason! I understand why you're upset, and I know you're hurting!"

"Then give me what I need."

"We can work this out. I know we can," she says. "I have so much compassion for you."

"Then fuck me."

Marilyn struggles. As Jason unfastens his pants she feels around frantically behind her for her knapsack, finds it in the sink, and reaches inside. She grasps the knitting needles. She hesitates. But suddenly she feels his hand begin to pull down her underwear, and in her panic nothing matters but stopping him, stopping this right now. She thrusts the needles hard up under his ribs.

He backs up a step, looks at her in shock, then down at the needles and the blood.

She looks at him, horrified, and then at the blood on her hands, and then back at him as he crumples to the floor. She shouts through sobs, "God damn it, Jason! God damn it! I can't believe you'd do this to me! Fuck! *Fuck Fuck Fuck*! You were my *friend*!"

CHAPTER 6

Gina and Brigitte are sitting in Gina's kitchen, eating cake.

Gina says, "Oh my goddess. This is exquisite. I'm having a religious experience."

Brigitte responds, "I knew you'd love it!"

"What's in the layers, raspberry?"

Marilyn bursts in the back door, slams it, and with her head down walks into the kitchen and quickly past them.

Brigitte says, "And hazelnut!"

Gina holds out a fork to her daughter. "Marilyn, sweetie, you must try this!"

Marilyn doesn't look at them. "Later, Mom! I'll be in my room!"

Her mother says, "Hold on there. Where's the fire? Stop and say hello properly."

Marilyn stands in the doorway to the living room, with her back to them. She says, her voice shaking, "Hi, Mom! Hi, Brigitte! I've had a rough day and I want to freshen up in my room. Okay?"

Gina says, "Turn around and let me see you."

"Later, okay? Can I go now?"

"Now, young lady. Come here," Gina says, concerned.

Marilyn slowly turns around. Her eyes are red, and she has bruises on her neck. Her shirt is held together with bent paper clips.

Gina is on her feet instantly and goes to Marilyn. Brigitte stands too, and hovers.

Gina demands, "What happened?"

Marilyn starts to cry. She says, "Mom, Brigitte. You were right."

"Right about what?" Gina asks.

Marilyn, through the tears, says, "About . . . talking to . . . It doesn't work."

"Who? Talking to who?"

"To . . . you know . . ."

Gina grabs Marilyn's shoulders and cries, "What? What happened? What happened, honey?"

Brigitte says, "Oh my god. Who was it? *I will kill him. I will kill him!*"

Gina turns to Brigitte and says, "That's *my* job." She turns back to Marilyn and says, tenderly, "Sweetie, oh, no, are you okay? Oh, god, of course you're not okay. Tell me what happened. We're going to the hospital right now. Come on, sweetie." She puts her arm around her daughter.

Marilyn responds, "No, no. I'm okay. He didn't actually do it."

"Thank god!" Gina says as Brigitte says, "Thank goddess!"

Marilyn takes a deep breath. "He tried. He tried really hard. I stopped him. I stopped him before he could . . ."

Brigitte and Gina think a moment before Brigitte says, "I thought you said talking didn't work."

Gina asks, "How did you stop him?"

Marilyn takes her knapsack off her shoulder, reaches inside, and pulls out two knitting needles smeared with blood.

Gina's eyes widen, and she takes Marilyn in her arms and hugs her hard. She says, "Oh, baby."

Brigitte yelps, "Your first kill!"

Gina looks at Brigitte, annoyed, and says, "That's

inappropriate! This is my daughter we're talking about!"

Marilyn nods, steels herself, and says, "That's right, I am your daughter. And I'm ready to join the knitting circle."

Tears spring into Gina's eyes. "You protected yourself. I'm so proud of you. And now you're ready to protect others. I'm just *so* proud of you!"

Brigitte asks, "What about the scene? You've removed the weapon; that's good thinking. Do we need to go and remove any fingerprints? Did anyone see you?"

Marilyn responds, "My friend Chrissy saw me after school, but she'd never tell. I know she wouldn't. And I knew enough to leave no trace of myself. I haven't eavesdropped on you all those times for nothing."

They all laugh. Then Brigitte says, "Come, darling, have some cake. You could use it."

They go to the table. Brigitte serves Marilyn a slice of cake, and Marilyn starts eating.

Then Gina says, "Marilyn, I want to go back to something you said earlier, just for a minute."

Marilyn is slightly cautious, in a way most daughters and sons are when their mothers make these sorts of loaded statements. She is silent.

"You made one remark in particular that I want to be sure we don't forget."

Marilyn's curiosity wins over her caution. "What?"

"You said, and I quote, 'Mom, you were right.'"

Brigitte adds a correction: "It was 'Mom, Brigitte. You were right.'"

Marilyn rolls her eyes, says, "Whatever."

Gina continues, "No, seriously. Let's write that down on the calendar so we never ever forget. 'Mom, you were right.'"

She smiles. "I like the sound of that."

Brigitte and Nick sit in Brigitte's living room. No music plays. They sit on her couch, each slightly facing the other. Brigitte holds Nick's hand in both of hers. She says to him, "I appreciate that you want to help . . ."

Nick responds, "I care about the issue. It's important for men to act in solidarity. And I care about you."

Brigitte smiles, a little sadly, and says, "Maybe that's my problem. You know I love you. But sometimes I worry we'll get too close."

"Really? What are you afraid of?"

"It's not a fear. I'm just concerned that if we get more entangled in each other's lives, then being together will start to become a habit."

Nick nods, then says, "And from there it becomes an obligation, and then, bingo, there goes the magic."

Brigitte's smile loses its sadness. "Exactly."

Nick says, "That's one of the things I love about you."

"Good!"

He continues, "The last thing I'd want is for us to turn our wonderful time together into a task, a duty."

"Good," she says.

"A stultifying obligation," he continues.

"Agreed."

"An achingly boring slog . . ."

"Okay!" Brigitte cuts him off, annoyed.

Nick says, "We're on the same page . . . Cutie."

Brigitte smiles again, says, "Cutie."

"But that doesn't mean I can't help. I can do something on my own, without you. You can give me an assignment. I'll be the

Undercover Secret Agent Lone Wolf, or something."

"I might be able to think of an assignment more easily if I get a back rub . . ."

Nick puts his free hand over hers. "Let's start the undercover work now!"

The members of MAWAR are at their headquarters, sitting around an old linoleum-topped kitchen table patterned with faded boomerangs. The stuffed squirrel and plastic monkey watch as the members play Bible Scrabble, where the only plays allowed are words or names found in the Good Book. This means wimpy secular words like *exegesis* or *queue* are not allowed. Further, words used in some versions of the Bible and not others can be worth less or more points. For example, words like *groovy* found only in *Good News Bibles* from the late 1960s ("And God saw everything that he had made, and behold, it was all so very groovy") are worth half points. Over the years there have been significant arguments over whether the word *debts* should count identically to the word *trespasses*. And certain words are because of their importance given triple value, words like *smite*, *know* (wink, wink), *sin*, and of course *crucifixion*. Another special rule is that anyone who plays the word *God* and loses the game (in other words, uses that name in vain) suffers consequences in games foreverafter.

This particular game sees a friendly yet fierce competition among four MAWAR men. But the tone of the contest changes dramatically when Billy Bob puts down tiles that spell *Jezebel*. Their leader looks up from his rack, where he'd been trying to spell *Hezekiah* (Bible Scrabble has a lot more Zs, and also blank tiles which are not used as wild cards but instead as alternative ways to spell You Know Who's name without everlasting *consequences*). Seeing the name *Jezebel* takes their leader's mind off the game. He demands of Zebadiah, "Why hast thou not consummated the plan to capture that heathen ditz?"

Zebadiah looks away.

Their leader says, "Didst the heathen call after you sent your holy fucking text message?"

Zebadiah still cannot look at him, but does nod curtly.

"What sayeth she?"

"She said she bought some new sho—"

"Leaveth thee off the bit about the fucking shoes, and get thee to the meat of it."

Zebadiah says, "She . . ." He trails off, turning bright red.

Their leader presses hard. "She sayeth what?" He stands. He moves around the table to stand next to Zebadiah. He insists, "What didst that Jezebel say?"

Zebadiah juts out his chin, then says, defiantly, "Her name is Jasmine, and I'd prefer you not call her Jezebel."

All the men of MAWAR gasp, and stand as one. They surround Zebadiah, move in very close. He shrinks in his chair (while still covering his rack; he had a very nice Zamzummims stashed away for next turn), begins to sweat.

All of the men point at him with quivering, accusing fingers.

He wishes he were somewhere else, someone else.

Together they begin to chant, at first slowly, and then with more speed and intensity, all in a sing-song voice, "Zebadiah and Jezebel—"

He interrupts by shouting "Jasmine!"

They chant over him, "Sitting in a tree, K-I-S-S-I-N-G. First comes love, then comes marriage, then comes six Zebadiahs and six Jezebels—"

"Her name is Jasmine!"

"—in a baby carriage."

They stop. They are silent for a moment before their leader says, "Ah, he's shy. Mr. Nads of Steel hath fallen under the spell of Jezebel." They all laugh.

Zebadiah cries, "Her name's Jasmine!"

Later, after Bible Scrabble is finished, the leader comes to Zebadiah privately, and says, "So, are you going to moveth our plan forward?"

Zebadiah says, "Yes, sir. But it is so scary."

"The plan is scary?"

"No, sir."

"What these horrible women are wroughting on the world as we know it is scary?"

"No, sir. I mean, yes, sir, that is very scary."

"But that's not it, is it?"

"No, sir."

"We both know what it is that hath frightened thou, don't we?"

"Yes, sir. It is love. Love is very scary."

"There are cures for love, you know."

"Like marriage?"

"That's one. Intimacy is another. Friendship. Getting to know the other person. Conversation. All those doth surely kill love. So there is yet hope. Just talk to her a little while, brother Zebadiah, and your feelings will go away. Trust me on this one."

"Thank you, sir. This helps, but still I feel so weak in the face of this love, and the temptations this love can bring."

"You may be weak, but Jesus hath strength enough for all of us. And remember, he lived thirty-three years and never knew a woman, never was intimate, never was in love. Let him be an example to you, and to us all. Let him be your strength. Let him be your holy fucking nads of steel."

Zebadiah doesn't say anything.

The leader says, "Mindest thou if I speak explicitly?"

"No, please do."

"Remember always that Jesus can help us in any circumstances, no matter how troubling. And he can help us with our sexuality, even though he died a virgin, blessings to him and to his blessed unused genitals."

"He can help us, truly?"

"He can help us no matter what our trouble. Sometimes, even though I am married, when I see some woman other than my wife, my Peter doth still become a Rock; when that doth happen I think of Jesus on the Cross, and before you know it, I can tie my Peter in a knot and pee sideways. And Jesus helps me in the other direction, too. Sometimes with my wife it is not always easy to fulfill my husbandly duties. . . ."

"I don't understand, sir."

"Let's just say that Peter is not always the Rock upon which my church is founded. In those cases, even though I am with my wife, sometimes instead of thinking of her I picture the precious face of Jesus, I picture the flowing robes, I picture us breaking bread and drinking wine as we lean against each other at the Last Supper, and the Next to Last Supper, and the Supper Before That. I picture us walking hand in hand through the garden, I picture a gentle kiss (with no awkward consequences like some *other* kiss in the garden) with that sweet, sweet Man, and before you know it, Lazarus has been raised from the dead."

"You do this, sir?"

"I do. And I think a lot of other people do, too. Why do

you think that so many people, when they are having sex, cry again and again, 'Oh, Jesus! Oh my God! Oh, Jesus!'?"

Zebadiah sits in the dimly lit, lonely basement office of MAWAR. He is confused. What used to be clear is now muddled. The Knitting Circle must be stopped, and the way to stop the Knitting Circle is to kidnap Jasmine and hold her hostage. But his feelings are getting in the way. It's not that he particularly objects to snatching her; snatching her is necessary for the plan to succeed. He doesn't even particularly object to snatching someone he likes. The problem is that now that he likes her, he finds himself too scared to even talk to her.

He thinks on his predicament, and reflects on the wise words given by his wise leader, "Let Jesus be your strength." So, what would Jesus do in these circumstances? What would Jesus do if he were planning to kidnap a woman in order to force her knitting circle to stop killing rapists? What would Jesus do if he met this woman in a nightclub called Xanadu, and if Jesus called the woman "fox-ay," and this woman really was pretty hot, and if Jesus started to like her, but then found himself too scared and tongue-tied to pull off the kidnapping? What would Jesus do then?

Zebadiah looks around the room, takes in the fusty drapes concealing a window that has been nailed shut, the Jesus-on-a-String Mountain Breeze cherry-kiwi air freshener, the desk, the computer, the telephone, the print on the wall of Jesus emerging from the grave, the twenty-five-year-old cheesecake calendar for a defunct tire company. What would Jesus do in this room?

Zebadiah looks again around the room and thinks about his beloved Jesus. He pictures Jesus being reborn—pictures Jesus having lived not only two thousand years ago but getting a chance at a second life right now!—and imagines Jesus walking around the room in his flowing robe and sitting down at the desk (first running his hand over his bottom to smooth out his robe). All at once, Zebadiah knows exactly what he needs to do.

Meanwhile the knitting circle continues to grow.

Men are starting to join, too.

On garlic cheddar day a man walks quietly into the knitting circle meeting, nods to the women, sits down, and begins knitting a very thin, long piece that doesn't look like any item of clothing the other knitters have ever seen before. It is a gorgeous cerulean. He comes back the next week, and the week after, and the week after. Eventually, his knitted whatever-it-is trails down and coils in a pile on the floor. In all that time he does not say a word.

Finally, Brigitte has to know. "What are you knitting? That's too long and skinny even for a scarf."

The man holds up a knitted rope. He says, "In my case, it was my teacher."

Christine says, "I'm so sorry, dear."

Mary looks at the rope and says, "But it's *very* nice knitting. Very even."

And Jasmine: "I adore that color."

Picture this: a man is in his library. An impressive selection of books lines the walls. They signify a fine intellectual mind, the mind of a learned man, the mind of someone worthy of passing his wisdom to the next generation. (He has not read most of them, but let's ignore that—mentioning it would be uncharitable.) This man wears a tweed jacket. It has leather patches on the elbows. This style choice also signifies a fine, highly developed intellect. Everybody knows that all the best teachers wear this kind of jacket. He also wears a knitted rope. This rope weaves its way around his hands, binding them tightly together, and around his neck, and around the base of the chandelier in this man's fine library. This rope is cerulean. The man's feet do not touch the floor.

People who aren't direct victims are joining, too.

A tall scrawny man wears a sleeveless leather jacket. From shoulder to wrist his arms are a writhing mass of tattoos. His hair is long and stringy, and his hairline is receding. He has a full beard and mustache and is missing an incisor and a canine. Though the day is overcast, he wears sunglasses. Beneath his leather jacket he wears a T-shirt that once was white. Around his neck is a braided leather thong, from which dangles a single bear claw.

He strides into the room (which smells of Roquefort cheese), throws bloody knitting needles onto the table, and declares, "He did my little sister."

Gina hurriedly takes a pair of disposable rubber gloves from her purse, puts them on, picks up the knitting needles, sterilizes them and with alcohol (which she also happens to carry in her purse), and hands the needles back to him. She says, "Proper cleanliness prevents disease. Have a seat, hon."

The man takes the cleaned needles, sits down, and starts knitting expertly—red mittens, if you must know.

Franz Maihem, who looks like a jumping spider, except that jumping spiders have eight legs and are actually kind of cute (and also have far more interesting and egalitarian courtship patterns), stares into the television camera (with only two eyes, as opposed to the jumping spider's eight; his eyes also see only three primary colors, as opposed to the four seen by jumping spiders, meaning their sensory color space is four-dimensional—but apart from that, and the fact that he can't jump several times his body length, oh, and also the fact that jumping spiders are by nature inquisitive and courageous, he is just like a jumping spider), and says, "This is Franz Maihem with ultraurgent breaking news. We are linking you live to our FBI contact Chet Stirling for an emergency announcement. Chet, go ahead."

Chet stands at his desk for several awkward seconds, staring blankly at the camera as the audio delay ticks by. Then his voice crackles as he says, "We have received a communiqué from the so-called Ice Queen Killers, whom our agency has classified as the greatest terrorist threat facing America today. They are more dangerous than al-Qaeda, the Taliban, North Korea, or Iran. They are even more dangerous and ruthless than domestic environmentalists. They are our top priority and we pledge to eradicate them."

Franz asks, "What does the communiqué say, Chet?"

"It says, 'We will stop killing rapists when men stop raping.'"

Franz asks, "That's it?"

"That's it. The entire message."

Franz asks, "What the heck does it mean, Chet?"

Chet responds with the uncertainty of a man standing waving his arms while he cries, "Where's my ass?": "Well, Franz, we're baffled. We have no idea what this could possibly mean. It's certainly shocking and depraved, but you know chicks, I mean women—they're incomprehensible."

"What do women want? That's the age-old question, isn't it, Chet?"

"Yes. We've done extensive research on this question, and experts concur that women are irrational, hysterical, and contradictory. They often say *no* when they mean *yes*. In fact, sometimes they're saying *no* with their mouths at the exact moment their eyes, and often their tantalizing breasts, are saying *yes*. They are devious, manipulative, lying, cheating, slutty whores."

Franz clears his throat. "The message, Chet?"

Chet regains his composure, such as it is, and says, "Cryptologists are urgently trying to decipher this message as we speak. As soon as we figure out its precise meaning, we'll alert the public. Meanwhile, please remain vigilant and report any suspicious activity."

The chief summons the remaining police to the war room. The police find the walls lined with large cardboard boxes. The chief is sitting at a table spread with Captain Marvel comics.

Flint points at the boxes. "What are these, Chief?"

The chief says, "I can't stop thinking about that message from the killers: 'We will stop killing rapists when men stop raping.' And I just can't understand what it could possibly mean. My thirty-five years, six months, and two weeks' experience as a police officer tells me this message is the key to stopping these murders."

"What does that have to do with these boxes?"

"That's where my extensive library of textbooks on different modes of detective theory and practices comes in so handy." He waves his hand over his desk, asks, "What do you see?"

"A bunch of comic books."

"That, Flint, is why I'm behind this desk and you are standing kind of off to the side at an angle. How do you think I got to be chief?"

"Because your father was chief, and also because both you and he gave lots of money to poll workers at the stations where you pulled in 175 percent of the vote."

"Besides that, how do you think I got to be chief?"

"Was it the 'get out of jail free' cards you handed to your primary donors and supporters?"

"Those are nice looking cards, aren't they? But besides that."

"The death threats against opponents?"

"Well, that, too, but besides all of those."

"I have no idea."

"Which is why you are there and I am here. I'll tell you. It's because I work my ass off to keep educated on both classic and modern practices of detection. Just last night I learned by reading *Encyclopedia Brown* how to consistently stop a bully named Bugs Meany. And then the night before I learned of the importance of always listening to Lassie. God knows how many times Timmy would have died if people hadn't learned to listen."

"I'm not following, sir."

"I'll make it clear: if this message is in code, we need to look at the techniques used by the world's expert code-ologist. And who is that?" He points at the comics, and says, "It's Captain Marvel, who at one time supplied the entire nation's next generation of potential police chiefs with secret decoder rings."

"I still don't see what this has to do with the boxes, sir."

The chief sighs heavily. "It would be too much to expect that people in this room kept their old Captain Marvel secret decoder rings, which means we'll have to work with what we've got."

"And what we've got . . ."

". . . Is about forty cases of Cracker Jacks bought with department money. We need to bre~k this message. I want some decoder rings, and I want them now. Dig in, boys."

Flint asks, "Do we have to eat all the Cracker Jacks?"

The chief responds, "Of course. Cracker Jacks, son, are one of the basic food groups."

Another cop says, "Uh, chief, I've bought these for my children. They don't actually contain prizes anymore, but instead little riddles. It's cheaper that way."

The chief, having already opened a box of Cracker Jacks, says, mouth full of caramel-covered popcorn and peanuts, "Well, shit. When will we ever get the break we need to solve these crimes?"

CHAPTER 7

Jasmine and Suzie are at Jasmine's great-grandmother's nursing home. It is the weekly Roller Derby Day, so they've brought bandages.

Great-grandmother Ahn didn't get off too bad this time: a couple of bruises on her arm and a bump on her forehead, "where that nasty piece of business Robin Banks hit me with a folding chair when I was about to lap her."

Jasmine gasps, "You need to get a new roommate, Grandma. That's too much."

Grandma Ahn says, "She's a nasty piece of business, all right. But all the other inmates are worse."

Jasmine and Suzie attend to her wounds, watch video highlights of that afternoon's game, compliment Grandma Ahn on her ability to fend off blockers with her walker, and jeer at Ms. Bank's perfidy. The three of them note with glee that Ms. Banks was sent off to do penalty time for the incident with the chair.

After that Grandma Ahn gives them a play-by-play of yesterday's bingo games, including detailed descriptions of the increasingly disgusted looks on Ms. Banks's face each time Grandma Ahn shouted Bingo just as Ms. Banks was taking in her breath to do the same. Grandma Ahn lowers her voice: "I think that's why she hit me with a chair." She covers her mouth and giggles.

Suddenly she stops giggling and asks without preamble, "Did you bring me any doughnut holes?"

Suzie says, "Of course," and begins rummaging in her backpack.

Grandma Ahn hisses, "Hurry. Get them to me before *she* gets back. If she sees them she'll want some, and if I don't give her any she'll take them as soon as I leave the room."

Suzie finds them and hands them over.

Grandma Ahn pops a couple in her mouth, then carries the bag to her bed, where she lifts a corner of the mattress, slides the treasure beneath, and lets the mattress fall back down. She returns to her chair and asks, again without preamble, "You have a boyfriend?"

Jasmine opens her mouth to speak.

Before she can answer, Grandma Ahn asks, gently, "Girlfriend?"

Jasmine inhales so she can say something.

But before she gets the words out, her great-grandmother says, "Makes no matter to me what you prefer, so long as the other person's not a nasty piece of business. That's what I told your grandmother and that's what I told your mother, and that's what I'll tell you, too, right now. Better to be alone than that."

Jasmine says, with meaning, "I've found someone very special."

"You have?" Suzie says.

"I told you about him."

"Who?"

"The One."

"Which one?"

Grandma Ahn asks, "What are you girls talking about?"

"The one I met at the Xanadu."

Suzie asks, "Months ago? The one with the text message?"

Grandma Ahn asks, "What's a Zandoo? And what's a sex

message?"

"Text, Grandma. Text," Jasmine says.

Grandma Ahn continues, "Not that I have anything against sex, but when I was young we could send messages other ways, too."

Jasmine says, flustered, "We're not having sex, Grandma."

Her great-grandmother looks at her a moment, then asks, sincerely, "Why not? Life's a one-way trip and you're not young for very long." She pauses a moment, then says, "And sex is good. What I wouldn't give 'bout now for some quality naked time with a—"

Jasmine reddens. "Grandma! Can we talk about something else, please?"

Grandma Ahn says, "Where's my doughnut holes? Did Ms. Banks take them already?"

"They're under your mattress, Grandma, and Ms. Banks isn't back from rugby practice yet," Jasmine says.

"So, what's your boyfriend look like?" Grandma Ahn asks.

Jasmine answers, "Well, at first he looked like Brad Pitt. Then later he looked like George Clooney. More recently he usually looks like a dragon. And sometimes he looks like the cutest little wombat. Then I just want to squeeze him."

Suzie says, "Jaz, are you all right?"

Grandma Ahn turns to Suzie and asks, "Does this make any more sense to you than it does to me?"

Suzie responds, "Not at all."

Grandma Ahn says to Suzie, "Thank God. For a moment there I thought I was getting old and losing my mind." She thinks a second, then says, also to Suzie, now conspiratorially, "Sometimes I wonder about her father's side of the family. Oh, the stories I could tell about the Maias . . ."

Both Jasmine's and Suzie's eyes open wide as they try to think of something to say. They love Grandma Ahn, but once the family stories start. . . .

Instead, Grandma Ahn takes the subject back to The One. She turns to Jasmine and says, "I've heard of two-faced before, but this guy has four. It sounds to me like he's a nas—"

Jasmine says, "Look at the time! Gotta go, Grandma Ahn!"

After Suzie drops off Jasmine at her apartment, she calls Brigitte and asks if she can come over. Brigitte says yes, and soon the two are talking while listening to the soothing sounds of the multi-artist album *In Praise of the Trung Sisters*.

Suzie tells Brigitte of the conversation at the nursing home, leaving out references to roller derby, bingo, doughnut holes, Robin Banks, and Grandma Ahn's desire for quality naked time. She asks Brigitte what she thinks.

"He sounds like a nasty piece of business," Brigitte says.

"I'm really worried," Suzie says,

"Do you think he's abusing her?"

"It's not that," Suzie says. "I don't think he even exists."

"What do you mean?"

"I think," Suzie continues, "that Jasmine has an imaginary boyfriend."

Brigitte thinks a moment, then says, "I've had a few of those. And frankly some of them have been preferable to—"

Suzie cuts her off: "But you knew they were imaginary, right? You didn't tell your friends you'd met someone special, did you?"

"Houston," Brigitte says, "I think we have a problem."

Although the news media, the FBI, and the police all have a difficult time deciphering the meaning of the knitting circle's message—"We will stop killing rapists when men stop raping"—many other people seem to understand it very well.

Knitting circles begin springing up all around the country.

Picture women walking together down a side street (or rather, *the* side street) in Horn Hill, Alabama, trailing long knitted scarves behind them. Picture other women (and a few men) doing the same in Central Park. Picture women on beaches in Hawaii wearing knitted bikinis and matching scarves. Picture women deer hunting near Beaver Creek, Montana, wearing bright orange vests and caps knitted from the finest angora. Picture college students carrying knitted backpacks, and businesswomen carrying knitted briefcases. Picture knitted helmet covers and footie boot covers worn by biker gangs. Picture pirates flying knitted flags with a skull and crossed needles instead of bones. Picture knitted flowerpot covers, knitted toilet seat covers (and I guarantee the seat gets raised and lowered properly in these households). Picture a group of women sneaking into the Lincoln Memorial to lay a knitted scarf around The Great Emancipator's neck.

Picture people giving their loved ones gifts of sweaters. Picture a high school boyfriend and girlfriend sharing a sweater made for two. Picture knitted sweaters keeping dogs warm, keeping cats warm, keeping horses and cows and pigs and chickens warm. Picture a field of sheep wearing brightly colored sweaters.

Or picture this. A man ambles down a dusty deserted country road. He is carrying a fishing pole and whistling the *Mayberry Theme*. Suddenly four women brandishing knitting needles step out from behind trees. The man stops. You can see the terror in his eyes. He stutters, "W-w-who sent you? Was it Becky?"

Silence from the women.

He asks, "Amy?"

More silence from the women.

"Patricia?"

Still more silence.

He sighs heavily. "I'm not really helping my own cause, am I?"

Or picture an office building late at night, where a different group of knitting-needle-wielding women approaches a frightened man. He backs away and they walk relentlessly toward him. You know what he has done to these women. You know that the moment of accountability is near. They stalk him through a maze of cubicles until they corner him in a conference room. You cannot bear to watch. You look away. You hear his scream, and the scream suddenly silenced.

Through the open doorway you see a ball of lavender yarn roll across the floor.

Or picture this: A man breaks into a woman's home while she is sitting in her living room, reading a book. Her knitted handbag is at her side. He enters the room and she jumps, startled, then regains her composure. He looms. He smiles menacingly as he reaches for her. She stands and sneers at him, "You wanna fuck with me? Okay. You wanna play rough? Okay. Say hello to my little friend!" She pulls out the biggest knitting needle you've ever seen, and the last one this man will ever see.

Or picture this. A woman runs down a dark alley, looking behind her. A man runs in hot pursuit. The alley ends at a fence topped with razor wire. The woman turns and faces the man. She sticks her hand into her purse. The man stops, out of reach, and watches her. The woman says, "I know what you're thinking. Does she have knitting needles, or does she not? Well, to tell you the truth, in all this excitement I kind of lost track myself. But being as you have no idea, you've got to ask yourself one question: 'Do I feel lucky?' Well, do ya, punk?"

The man says nothing.

The woman continues, a smirk developing on her face, "Come on, make my day."

Or picture this: A woman walks through a deserted parking garage that looks like almost every deserted parking garage that almost every woman has ever walked through alone late at night. The tap tap tap of the woman's heels echo off concrete walls. She looks around nervously.

A man erupts from behind a pillar, confronts her. "Don't worry," he sneers. "I'm not going to rape you. I'm just going to kill you." He pulls out a knife and waves it in the air. He's quite good, as impressive in his own way as Riversong was with his scarves. He begins by holding the knife high, like a banderillo holding his banderilla in preparation for tormenting the bull. Then he windmills his arm a couple of times, like Pete Townshend or a fast-pitch softball pitcher, or like Pete Townshend playing softball. He tosses the knife from hand to hand, then does the same behind his back. He throws the knife in the air, the blade whirling, and catches it in his teeth.

The woman notices old scars on his face.

He grips the knife in his hand, and begins to move towards her.

Before he can get too close, the woman whips a knitting needle out of her bag. The man stops, curious. She repeats his routine, matches him move for move, except for the one where he flipped the knife in the air and caught it with his teeth. She does, however, make a mental note to try this out at home (wearing protective glasses and face gear for safety, of course).

The man says, "Very impressive. But I'm still going to kill you." He pulls a sword from behind the pillar. He points it at her and performs an Arabesque *onlair*, followed by a stunning series of lightning fast pirouettes, finishing with a magnificent *tour jeté*, or more formally, a *grand jeté dessus en tournant.*

He advances upon the woman again, sword ready to thrust. She holds up her hand. He stops again, curious. She pulls a gun from her jacket pocket, aims, and shoots him in the forehead. He falls like a sack of potatoes. She notes, "Foolish consistency is the hobgoblin of little minds."

Or picture this: A company of women stand in the full parking lot of "Little Willie's House of Wanking: Get a Beer When You Buy a Spanking!" One of the women shouts, "Present Arms!" The women stand to attention, needles at the ready. Another woman commands, "Forward, march!" The women start toward the building in a trim line. Yet another woman calls out, "Double time!" The line surges forward.

Then you hear it. First one woman, and then another, and then another, begins to keen a battle cry, until the night fills, then explodes with the screams and yells of their mothers and grandmothers and great-grandmothers; fills, then explodes with the rage and frustration and sorrow of thousands of years of taking it and taking it and taking it, and the joy of finally fighting back. The sound is purely human, purely animal. The sound is the sound of no turning back.

When the women are done, the building is gone.

So are its customers.

The enormous popularity of knitting circles and the consequent disappearance of so many rapists cannot but affect society as a whole.

Picture this: football players trot gamely onto a field, despite the fact that there are only three players per team. Happy cheerleaders on the sidelines wear sporty new sweaters.

Or picture this: a boxer swings at no opponent, then raises his hands high over his head in victory. Of the very few people in the crowd, most are women knitting. The referee hands the champion a knitted belt.

Or this: a baseball player pitches to an empty home plate, then walks in and picks up the ball. He picks up a bat, tosses the ball and swings. A pop fly! He's under it, he's got it, he catches it, he's OUT!

Or this: A guy shows up to a frat house party. Woo! But wait, where's the thumping music? Where are the strobe lights? Where are all kegs? Where are all the drunken girls who have been plied with alcohol until they're ready for action (i.e., barely conscious)? He enters the quiet room. PAR-TAY! Woo! Woo! He glances around nervously. This guy is a survivor. He's not stupid (at least, not in that way. Confidentially, he's not the brightest student ever to grace the university. But he is smart enough to have lived this long, and that's saying a lot, considering the company he used to keep). He approaches the bar and pours himself a nice tall glass of milk. He sinks into the couch in the room formerly known as the make-out lounge, alone. He drums his fingers. He grins—he hasn't had this much fun in weeks!

Or this: a man in an Air Force uniform looks at a radar screen. He sees a blip, picks up a phone. He shouts, "Enemy airplane observed. Prepare defenses!"

He stands, runs downstairs, out the building, and over to an antiaircraft gun. He picks up a phone. He shouts, "Ready to fire, sir! From which direction is the aircraft coming?"

He runs back into the building, upstairs, over to the radar

screen, picks up the phone. He shouts, "From the west. Fire when ready!"

He runs back downstairs, then slumps exhausted over his antiaircraft gun.

Or picture this: a soldier huddles in a trench. He removes a medallion from around his neck, closes his eyes, and kisses it. He hangs it on the side of the trench. He hears a voice shout, "Charge!" He leaps out of his trench and into no-man's land. He rushes across. He is alone. He reaches the trench on the other side. It is empty. He throws his arms in the air, shouts to the heavens, "We won!" He pauses, then adds, "I think."

Or picture this: a group of middle school students crowd around their male teacher's desk. A female teacher stands nearby. One of the girls tells the male teacher, "We want to start a knitting club after school."

He responds, "Um. I'm not sure that would be a good idea."

The female teacher interjects, "Yes, that's a very nice idea, girls."

The girls cheer.

Or this: a father teaches his little daughter how to hold a needle. She concentrates, determined to get it right. He says, "Hold it like this, and then thrust upward between the ribs. It's all in the execution, as it were."

Or this: A man holds in his hands his birthday present. It is in a box smaller than Pandora's box, but certainly bigger than Mama's squeezebox. He looks at it with anticipation, like a little boy about to open a, well, present. He rips off the paper, tears open the box, and sees . . . a hand-knit sweater. He blanches, then looks fearfully at his wife.

She asks innocently, "Don't you like it, dear?"

All creatures respond to positive and negative reinforcement. It does not take long for men to begin to understand and respond to the message of the knitting circles.

It is a cold night. A burnt orange 2001 Pontiac Aztek is parked in an alley behind a Piggly Wiggly grocery store. The windows are steamed over. A man sits on the back seat, and a woman straddles him, moving mechanically up and down.

"This feels soooo good," the man says. He closes his eyes. "Baby, do you really like me, or are you just doing this for the money?"

The woman responds, her voice as mechanical as her movements, "I really like you, baby. I like you so much."

The man frowns, and gently pulls her off him. She settles next to him. He pulls his shirt down to cover himself and looks into her bored eyes. He says, "But will you still like me tomorrow?"

"Sure, I'll like you tomorrow, if you still got money."

"So . . . you wouldn't do this for free?"

The woman answers immediately, without thinking, "Are you out of your fucking mind?"

"Are you telling me you're doing this just for the money?"

"What'd you think, Jack? You think I wanna stand out here freezing my ass off waiting for losers like you to come and poke me?"

He says, "I thought you liked me."

"I like you when you got some money for me. Now let's hurry up, cuz mama's gotta make her living."

She tries to climb on top of him again. He holds her still. He says, "Wait. This is your job?"

She rolls her eyes. "Give the man a prize."

He asks, trying to puzzle his way through this, "Don't you like sex for its own sake?"

"Sure, I like sex, but that's not what we're doing here. This is called commerce."

The man looks nervous. "But it's not, you know, the R-word, is it? And you don't have any friends who, you know, knit, do you?"

She says, "Don't worry, Jack. You're not raping me. You're exploiting me. There's a difference, albeit one of degree rather than quality. They're on a continuum. I'm not doing this because I want to, but because I need the money. I'm forced by my economic circumstances, even if you're not personally forcing me, get it? But I'm not going to kill you, baby. I like your free-flowing cash too much."

"You're using me for my money?"

"Look. Women make, on average, in a normal job, 75 percent of what men make. Do the math. You try raising two kids on minimum wage. Now shut up and let me earn my eighty bucks."

Now the man is really concerned. He says, "I thought fifty was the going rate. . . ."

"The extra thirty," the woman responds, "is for the economics lesson."

Suzie is lying on her bed in her brand new apartment with her boyfriend Sam. They are both fully clothed. Sam is as gorgeous as is Suzie, who is as gorgeous as is Sam. Together they are as cute as a pair of chipmunks, as adorable as baby muskrats, as squeezable as baby bears (or maybe not), as lovely as a crashing stock market, as wondrous a sight to behold as a failing dam, as beautiful as a sharp kick in the . . . well, you know.

They gaze at each other with mad desire. Suzie reaches over to kiss Sam.

He pulls away.

She asks, "What's wrong? Don't you want to?"

He answers, "Desperately. But are you sure you want to?"

"More than anything!"

He asks, tentatively, "You're not going to . . . ?"

"What?"

"I saw you knitting earlier."

"Yes, kneepads for Jaz's Grandma Ahn's Roller Derby team. So?"

"It makes me nervous. What if you later decide that you didn't really want to, and that in some way—even some subtle way that I'm not aware of—I coerced you, or you felt coerced even if it wasn't my fault, and that therefore it was rape?"

Suzie cries, "I'm not going to do that! I'm dying for you! Isn't that clear enough?"

"I'm dying for you too! But how can you be sure?"

"I just am," she says. "I'm mad with lust for you."

He responds, "I'm mad with lust for you, too. Oh my god."

They look deep into one another's eyes, bring their faces closer and closer together. She closes her eyes, slightly parts her lips.

But he is a third-year philosophy major, and as such does not seem to understand that there are times for words and times to shut up. He says, entering full-on academic philosopher mode, "You may think you want to, but there might be underlying social and political forces affecting you psychologically that you're not aware of. I need to know if you want to want to."

Suzie opens her eyes slowly, sighs, then says, "Yes. I want to. I want to want to. I want to want to want to."

"But," Sam says, really getting up his philosophical steam, indeed his philosophical high dudgeon, or to put it another way, having gotten his philosophical knickers in a twist (instead of getting his knickers the way they're supposed to be, which is off), "how do you know that what you want is really what you want, and isn't just what you've been told you want by a patriarchal culture?"

"I know what my body says. And my body says I crave you. I craaaave you."

Sadly, once a philosopher gets a hold of an idea (as opposed to a body), it can be hard to get him to let go. He says, "I believe that you believe you crave me. But I'm worried about how much free will we really have in a culture as utterly coercive in every aspect as this one is, and how untainted our desires can really be.

"If we grow up believing in culturally constructed gender binaries and their coexistent roles, if we grow up in heteropatriarchy, indeed if we grow up immersed in compulsory heterosexuality—shaped by these ideas, really— plus commercially distorted standards of beauty, plus grow up burdened by the overwhelming weight of thousands of years of the institutional oppression of women, and the social relations and power disparities that flow from that to infect every aspect of this culture, contaminating every personal interaction between men and women, and, for that matter, men and men, and women and women, and children and everyone, in countless ways, ways we often can't even perceive because we're so immersed in them, sort of like how fish are said not to think about water because it's just their world, then how can we be sure that our sexual feelings and desires in general, and the people we're attracted to in particular, and the intimate acts we believe we want to do with them, would be the same as they would be without all those influences? How can we be certain of what we truly want, deep in our hearts?"

Suzie does not reply.

Sam fears he may have somehow offended her. He says, softly, cutely (cute as a baby porcupine, though not so prickly), "Suzie?"

Still more silence.

More cutely still, he says, "Suzie?"

Suzie snores softly, as adorable as a baby panda.

Brigitte and Nick are at Brigitte's home. From her stereo come the soft sounds of Che Guevara singing: *I left my Kalashnikov in San Francisco.*

Nick pleads, "You promised to give me something to do! When will I receive my assignment? I want to experience the glory, the glamour, the adventure of the knitting circle."

Brigitte looks at him. "You haven't forgotten about it yet?" She sighs. "Okay. I have your first assignment, Mr. Secret Lone Wolf Undercover Agent. This is pretty easy, but has glory, adventure, and glamour up the wazoo. You're going to be in arms procurement."

Nick's eyes open wide.

Brigitte says, "I need you to obtain three sets of new knitting needles. No more, no less. Three. Got that?"

Nick responds, "Got it! Aye-aye, Captain!"

Brigitte smiles. "Wrong genre, sweetie."

Daisy's Craft Barn is the essence of Americana. It's as American as apple pie, baseball, the Fourth of July. It's as American as invading small Latin American nations. As American as bombing people in Southeast Asia, Africa, the Middle East.

As American as land theft from the indigenous. As American as a phony democracy where no matter whom you vote for, the corporations win. As American as "free trade" policies enforced by the largest military the world has ever seen. As American as the importation of cheap crap manufactured in sweatshops around the globe to fuel a meaningless and frenzied consumer culture.

Nick hides behind a building across the street from Daisy's. He wears a fedora, a trench coat, and sunglasses. As he peers around the corner at the front of the craft store, he hums the theme song from *Mission: Impossible.*

The coast seems clear. Nick is not quite sure what the coast not being clear would look like, failing machine-gun nests and rolls of concertina wire throughout the parking lot.

He glides around the corner and makes his way, hands in his pockets, to the front door. It opens automatically, with a whoosh and a blast of cold air. He peers inside before entering. The store has a farmyard motif, with bales of straw at the ends of the aisles and the sounds of chickens and ducks coming over the loudspeakers.

A greeter, wearing a straw hat and overalls, says to him, "Welcome to Daisy's Craft Barn! Can I help you find something?"

Nick replies, "No, thank you."

"Really, I can take you right where you want to go."

Nick mumbles in the negative and tries to walk away quickly.

The greeter follows, saying, "Whatever you need, we got it here in The Barn! What's your pleasure, partner?"

Nick says, "Go away! I just want to browse." When the greeter remains at his heels, Nick points toward the front door. "Look, a greeting emergency! Someone else is coming in the door, ungreeted! What will she think?"

The greeter turns toward the door, and Nick slips down an aisle. Once alone, however, he begins to regret his decision. Daisy's Craft Barn is huge: Notre Dame Cathedral huge, airplane hangar huge, aircraft carrier huge, Superdome huge, Grand Mosque huge, outer space huge, unbearably huge, agonizingly huge, with a vastness that exposes the emptiness of the human soul and leaves people feeling alone and vulnerable and needing to buy that special thread or Sculpey modeling compound to make them feel once again alive. Besides, Nick's commitment to pro-feminism only goes so far. Treat women well: of course. Not feel entitled to their bodies: naturally. Support them in their struggle against oppression: 100 percent. Procure arms for them in this struggle: you bet. Go with them to a craft store: not on your life. So he has no idea where to go.

Nick slinks around the store, peering around the edges of his sunglasses and over the straw bales at the ends of the aisles. He tiptoes past ceramic piggies and past bins of beads (formed of glass, crystal, wood, seed, semiprecious stone, plastic, moose dung, rhino horn, tiger penis, bone shard from St. Peter, ectoplasm from the ghosts of Arthur Conan Doyle, Charles Dickens, Abraham Lincoln, William James, and Robert Plant [despite Plant not yet being dead, except perhaps musically]), down aisle after aisle of scrapbook materials, from one hundred and seventy-five styles of albums to sixty-three kinds of adhesives to Cuttlebug, Cricut, Sissix, and Slice die cutting aids. After several miles of walking, Nick becomes thirsty, and after several miles more he begins to hallucinate. The chicken and duck sounds over the loudspeakers coalesce into a poultry choir clucking and quacking the Sons of the Pioneers version of "Cool Water":

All day I face the barren waste (quack quack)
Without the taste of water, cool water (cluck cluck)
Old Dan and I with throats burned dry (quackity quack)
And souls that cry for water, cool, clear, water (cock-a-doodle-doo).

Finally he staggers into the correct aisle. But even here his trials aren't over. Brigitte asked him to bring three sets of knitting needles, but she didn't specify country of origin. One bin says its needles are proudly supplied from sweatshops in Guatemala, hardened with the tears of tired little girls. Another says its needles are superior because they're from Vietnam and suffused with the suffering and anguish of young women there. Another claims its needles are the best because they're from China and have been factory tested by being used to poke workers who fall asleep before the end of their twenty-six-hour workdays. Down at the far end of the aisle (past three mirages of cool, clear water) Nick finds a bin marked "Union-made in the USA." These needles cost six times as much as all the others put together. Nick vacillates for a moment between doing the right thing and following the inexorable logic of capitalism, which would lead him to buy the lowest-cost needles, in this case needles hand-carved by slaves from the femurs of third world orphans (a *Wall Street Journal* article pinned to the front of the bin extols these particular needles as an example of the triumph of green capitalism: "These needles are both inexpensive and sustainably harvested from a nearly inexhaustible supply of third world orphans (TWOs). Further, capitalism itself functionally and systematically guarantees a yearly increase in TWOs, meaning we can maintain this way of living forever, with no fear of ridiculous scaremongering notions such as Peak Orphans."). Nick chooses the former.

But still he faces a problem. He asks himself, quietly, "How can Brigitte only want three pairs? That's nothing. I should get enough to make it worth the trip."

He scoops up two huge armfuls of hundreds of knitting needles, then starts the long trek back to the front counter, stopping a few times to make camp and softly sing songs of the trail (starting with "Git Along, Little Dogies" and ending with "Plastic Jesus"). Finally he arrives, weary, hungry, thirsty, bedraggled, having lost only about a fifth of the needles along the way.

The clerk, like the greeter, wears a straw hat and overalls. He asks, "How many sets is that, sir?"

Nick is too tired to speak. He drops them on the conveyor belt, and begins to count them one by one.

The clerk glances at him, glances at the needles, and glances at a police bulletin taped behind the counter that reads, "If anyone buys more than three sets of knitting needles, alert the authorities immediately."

The clerk says, "I have to . . . um . . . I might be able to get you a high-volume discount on these babies. I'm going to, um . . . discuss it with my manager. Don't move, partner. I'll be back in a jiffy. Don't move!"

At first, Nick thinks he's too tired to move anyway, but when he sees the clerk whispering to the manager and pointing at Nick, then sees the manager (wearing overalls and a John Deere baseball cap) slap down the clerk's hand before mouthing "Don't let him know," Nick feels adrenalin surge through his body, getting a far bigger burst of energy than he would have even by hooking himself to one of the by-now-ubiquitous-at-superstores automated intravenous Mountain Dew machines. The wolf within the Long Wolf Secret Agent comes alive. He becomes all instinct. He—or rather his body—decides to run. His arms scoop up the needles. The needles fly into the air in all directions, and fall with a clatter that wakes the dead in a cemetery three miles away (the dead take only a few weeks to fall back asleep, but in the meantime they remain indistinguishable from most of their neighbors, and certainly from all golf fans). His right hand maintains its death grip on five of them. He tries to run but his feet slip on needles rolling on the floor. Other customers stare at him, expressionless as they continue to chew their cud. He finds himself smiling and giving them a little wave. But this inattention to his feet costs him: he trips and falls flat on his face. He scrambles up and rushes from the store, clutching the five knitting needles in his sweaty fist.

At the exit, a security camera captures a grainy black-and-white image of his panicked face.

Outside the door, a security guard sits on a stool, holding a huge dripping Big Mac. He also has fries, an apple pie and a coke balanced on his lap. He takes a bite, then looks up slowly as Nick runs by. He says, mouth full, "Mmmf!"

He carefully puts each item of food down on the ground beside the stool and heaves himself to his feet. This takes a long time. No, longer than that. A really long time. No matter how long you are thinking this took, add about fifteen seconds to it, and that's how long it took.

Meanwhile, the clerk and manager race out the door, look around, see that the suspect has fled, and call 911 on a cell phone. They run back inside, ignoring the security guard, who finally straightens up and points in the direction the suspect ran.

The security guard shouts, "Hey! Stop!"

By chance, Sandy Dougher has been patrolling the neighborhood in her squad car. The radio crackles and she hears the voice of the dispatcher: "All units, we have a code ten on channel one, all units."

She hears Flint's voice: "I copy. Go ahead."

"The party is showing physical as white male, six foot, two twenty, brown and hazel. Break."

She hears the voice of another cop: "Go ahead."

Then the dispatcher: "Out of Daisy's Craft Barn. Suspect has fled on foot, going north on Main. He is armed and extremely dangerous. Break."

She hears Flint's voice again: "Go ahead."

Then the dispatcher, "We need to get this sucker. The perp is suspected, at minimum, of shoplifting and trafficking in knitting needles. He attempted to purchase a large volume of these weapons, and escaped in possession of several of them. Approach with extreme caution. Use force in accordance with departmental use of force policy. In other words, beat the fucker to a pulp before you shoot him. Do you copy? Break."

Sandy says, "I copy. I'm on it."

Then she hears Flint's voice, "I got here first, bleeder. I'll handle it."

Sandy mutters, "You're going to regret calling me that, you motherfucking pig—"

The dispatcher says, "What's that? I didn't copy that, Officer."

Sandy realizes she'd still been holding the transmit button on the radio extender. "I told Officer Stone I'd be honored to offer backup."

The two police cars race from opposite directions toward Daisy's Craft Barn, careening down streets and through alleys, sirens blaring.

The dispatcher says, "Your positions, Officers? Break."

Sandy hears Flint say, "I'm heading into the parking lot now."

The dispatcher: "Good. Officer Dougher?"

"I'm still half a mile from the scene," Sandy says.

"I said I'm on it. Go write some parking tickets, Dougher," Flint says.

At that moment, Sandy spots Nick, who is walking exaggeratedly casually along the sidewalk, whistling, hiding one hand inside his trench coat. Sandy says to the radio, "Go for it, Officer. You're obviously a better man than I."

"Damn straight," Flint says.

Sandy shakes her head in disgust, then makes absolutely sure her radio microphone is not transmitting before she adds, "And a colossal asshole."

Siren blaring and lights flashing, Flint races his car into the parking lot at Daisy's Craft Barn. He screeches to a stop, opens his door, and jumps out. He pulls out his gun and waves it around, causing terrified customers to scream and fall to the ground. He runs toward the store's door.

Nick pretends not to notice the police car driving right next to him. Driving *very* slowly right next to him. He pretends not to notice the police officer staring at him through the open passenger-side window. The *female* police officer staring at him. The quite attractive female police officer staring at him. The quite attractive female police officer who will probably put him in prison for the rest of his life. He pretends to notice none of this.

But what he really doesn't notice is the tree root that has buckled the sidewalk directly in front of him. He stumbles and puts both hands in front of him to break his fall, then regains his balance, if not his pride. At this point there's no way he can pretend not to notice the knitting needles that have clattered to the ground. He looks at the female police officer (the quite attractive female police officer, etc.), smiles, waves shyly.

She stops the car. "Better get in the back."

Nick ineptly picks up the knitting needles, wondering the whole time whether he'll be able to survive Hard Time in the Big House, probably working on the Rock Pile when he's not spending years in The Hole. Needles picked up, he gets into the back of the squad car, wondering if this will be the last time he experiences the sweet taste of liberty.

CHAPTER 8

Sandy doesn't put Nick into handcuffs, and doesn't even lock the door. She puts the car into drive and carefully accelerates. She says, "I'm going to remove you from the area. It's pretty hot around here."

Nick responds, "Whew, it sure is. Would you mind turning on the AC?"

"That's not what I meant, Nick," she says.

"You know who I am?"

"I've heard about you."

Despite his predicament, Nick is pleased. "You probably heard about my exploits as a Lone Wolf Secret Undercover Agent."

Sandy doesn't say anything. She drives for several miles—radio occasionally giving news of the pandemonium at Daisy's Craft Barn—then stops in the parking lot of a fast food restaurant. She gets out of the car and leans back inside to talk to Nick. She says, "I'm going to the bathroom. I'll be gone for three minutes. Wait right here. Don't open this unlocked door and run away to avoid arrest during the three minutes I'm leaving you unobserved."

She goes into the restaurant (if you can call it that).

When she returns, Nick says to her, "That was a lot longer than three minutes."

Sandy gets into the front seat and starts flipping through paperwork. She says, "Oops, I left your door unlocked and I forgot to put cuffs on you! You could probably escape if you ran fast. Or even if you jogged moderately quickly."

Nick holds out his hands for cuffs.

Sandy sighs. Then she says, "We'll try this one more time. Hit me. Make it look good. I mean bad."

Nick says, "Are you crazy? I could never hit a woman!"

Sandy, frustrated, rests her head on the steering wheel.

They hear the voice of the dispatcher, "Unit One, have you spotted the suspect yet? We have confirmed his identity as Nick Newman. We repeat the physical of white male, six feet, two twenty, so he's a tad chubby—"

Nick barks, "Am not!"

The dispatcher continues, "Brown and hazel. And not terribly handsome—"

Nick barks again, "Am so!"

The dispatcher continues, "He is armed with five knitting needles, and is therefore extremely dangerous. He is believed to be the terrorist mastermind behind the Ice Queen Murders. Deadly force is in order. Don't even pause to beat him up—just shoot him on sight."

Sandy's and Nick's eyes lock in the rearview mirror. He looks terrified, and makes a little whimpering noise.

Sandy says, "What the hell do I have to do to help you escape? Run, you idiot!"

Nick runs down the street to Brigitte's house, still clutching the five knitting needles. His hat is gone, as are his sunglasses. His trench coat, by now drenched with sweat, flaps behind him. As he runs he occasionally looks behind him in a panic. But no one follows. He makes it to her door and taps furtively. From inside he hears the swing version of Nat Turner singing "I'm Dreaming of a Revolutionary Christmas."

Nick whispers, "Brigitte! Brigitte!"

There is no answer. He looks around to see if anyone has followed him. No one. He pounds harder. He yells, "Brigitte! Hey!"

No answer.

Nick goes around to the side of the house, peers in a window. He sees Brigitte in her living room, dancing, oblivious to him. He taps on the window, then waves. She doesn't see him. He knocks harder on the glass, taps it with the needles. No luck. He picks up a stone and taps with that, finally breaking the window. He looks shocked. She lets out a startled yelp and sees him. He waves sheepishly.

She says, annoyed, "Holy crap, Nick. You could have knocked on the damn door."

Nick says, his voice thin with panic, "Let me in, Brigitte! Hurry, hurry! They're after me!"

She rushes to the door, opens it, and hustles Nick inside. "What? They're after you? For going to Daisy's Craft Barn?"

Nick hands her the five needles.

She takes them. "That's not three pairs. You're one short."

"I know! I lost them all! I had hundreds of pairs! But then they chased me! Oh my god. What am I going to do? Can I stay here until it all blows over?"

She blinks her eyes, not believing—or really even understanding—what she is hearing.

He continues, "Who am I kidding—it'll never blow over. You'll have to hide me here for the rest of my life. I'll be like Anne Frank, hiding up in the attic not saying a peep, and you'll bring me stale bread as I slowly go insane from boredom and isolation . . . What did you get me involved in?"

"What did I—*What?*—You—"

"Why did you make me do something so dangerous?"

Brigitte spits, "You begged me to give you something to do! I gave you a simple task, an easy task, something that no one could possibly fuck up!"

"Evidently it wasn't so easy after all, was it?" Nick says. He flicks on the television. "I want to see if it's in the news yet."

Chet Stirling is reporting: "Local police are reported to have had in their clutches the terrorist ringleader, the veritable Osama bin Laden of knitting needles. But the sly and dangerous terrorist slipped through their grasp, and remains at large. It was the man in this photo, which was taken by a security camera as he fled the scene of an attempt to illegally obtain weapons. We urge viewers to remain hiding in their homes, shaking in terror and consumed with paranoia, as long as this evil serial killer remains at large. Of course he turned out to be a man, a man with an analytical mind. Clever and devious, he had impersonated a group of women in an attempt to throw us off the scent, but we always knew that women couldn't possibly plan such an elaborate and multilayered scheme."

Nick looks at Brigitte, who is appalled by what she is now understanding. He says, smugly, "He called me 'clever.' Did you hear that? Clever."

Not just the police and MAWAR are opposed to the knitting circles. In fact many groups, large and small, from all across the political spectrum (running, as it nearly always does in this culture, from ludicrous on one end to absurd on the other), oppose them.

They are opposed, for example, by a significant portion of male anarchists. Anarchists claim they're against all forms of oppression, and many truly are, so you might think all anarchists would be in favor of people actively stopping rape. Sadly, such is not the case. Members of this particular subgroup of anarchists who oppose the knitting circles mean something different by "ending oppression" than do members of various knitting circles themselves. One of the major anarchist groups opposed to the knitting circles (if we measure "major" not by their numbers, which are minuscule, but rather by how vocal they are and by the pungency of their personal body odor, which is greater by far than the stinkiest of stinky cheeses; indeed, each year this particular brand of anarchists holds their own version of the Miss America contest, called the Crust Punk contest, wherein the dreadlocked and bearded male with the strongest smell and the thickest layer of crusted body excretions is crowned Un-King of the Anarchists by someone—anyone, please—who can stomach getting close enough to do so). These roving gangs of black-clad males, noted as much for their militantly casual approach to personal hygiene as for their contempt for any and all efforts to constrain what they call their Feral Edge Freedoms, roam the streets (by car when they can "borrow" their parents' gas cards, and by foot when they can't) looking for females (and failing that, inanimate objects) into whom they can inject their Revolutionary Ardor.

One night, several members of the AFACASISF emerge from their respective parents' basements to gather in the basement of one of their fellow "insurrectionist's" parents to "do some writing." When these anarchists tell the parents they'll be writing, the parents say first to the anarchists, "You can write?" and then say to themselves, "Thank god they won't be playing music tonight." The "musical style" of the anarchists' band (called Seppuku Suicide Hara-kiri, mainly because that's what it makes listeners want to do) is called deathvomitnoise. Because of the importance of their message (and also as a statement of their artistic integrity and because, as they say, "You can't improve on perfection, dude," but mainly because of laziness on the part of band members, and finally because no one would notice the difference anyway), all songs by Seppuku Suicide Hara-kiri have the same lyrics, which are screamed unintelligibly over the sounds of guitars being tortured: "Fuck, Fuck, Fuck, FUUUUUCCCCCCKKKKK. Fuckfuckfuck. Aaaaaahhhh. Fuck. Fuck you if you listen to this and fuck you if you don't. Fuck you. Fuck anyone who plays anywhere other than a basement. Fuck you if you have an audience, you oppressor. Fuck you. The shoe will drop and so will you, you fucking liberal sellout. Fuck. When the shoe drops the vomit of industry will spew. Shoe. Shoe. Drop the other shoe, motherfucker." The sounds of music coming from the basement normally make the parents look at each other wistfully, nostalgically longing for the early days of their marriage before their child was born. Nights the songs have driven them to too much to drink, the recriminations start with the mother saying, "I begged to be allowed to go down to Baby-B-Gone. It would have been, what, a few minutes of discomfort, then maybe or maybe not a few days of sadness, and a lifetime of freedom from the grinding horror of his music, and frankly from his personality (if you can call it that)." This leads to bitter words on the father's part, and then to a discussion about the only one of their son's band's songs they actually like, "My Mother Should Have Had an Abortion." The argument normally ends with the father saying those words so rare, so precious, coming from the man in the household: "You were right, and I was wrong."

But this night there is no deathvomitnoise, so the parents only ask themselves, "What *is* that smell?"

Tonight, the AFACASISF has a job to do. At the end of

the evening they post on the internet their defining "rant," to use their preferred word (these self-proclaimed Anarchist Pricks disavow the word *communiqué* as "too tainted by its association with bourgois [sic] liberal communist counter insurrectionary forces that attempt to inhibit our Feral Edge Freedoms." In this rant, entitled "The Politics of Impotence," these Anarchists "rale [sic] against" all those women who are oppressing them by attempting to impose some form of what these Anarchist Pricks derisively call "community norms." "How dare these women," the rant rhetorically asks, "play the gender card by attempting to force us to behave according to their entirely arbitary [sic] standards? Why do women get all this power? How dare they tell us what we can and cannot do with our own bodies? We will not take this insult—this authoritarianistic policing, this fascistic Nazi assault on our freedoms—laying [sic] down on our backs! These so-called knitting circle women are a ribbed condom on the throbbing cock of freedom, holding back the spontaneous expression and explosion of true and orgasmic insurrection!"

Fortunately, their website only gets thirty-five hits, thirty-three of which are by their own members, with the other two being by pasty-faced perverts who've done internet searches for the words "cock, throbbing, Nazi, and impotence." Nonetheless, they consider the rant a raving success.

Even more fortunately, the militantly casual approach to personal hygiene on the part of members of these Anarchist Prick Patrols not only alerts intended recipients of their feral ardor to their presence, allowing these most definitely unwilling recipients to escape, but also helps members of various knitting circles to find these rapists and turn the tables, or more accurately knitting needles, on them.

Unsurprisingly, the animal rights group PATE, People Against Treating Nonhuman Animals Execrably (who fully recognize the acronym should be PATNAE, but in a brilliant marketing move keep it as PATE so they can get free advertising anytime anyone mentions pâté), also comes out against the knitting circles.

The head of PATE, who has a bald one, issues a press release declaring, "This is a disaster for our animal companions and friends. If men aren't allowed to rape women, we know what this means for the pigs, cows, sheep, bunnies, and chickens of the world. We cannot stand by and allow this horrible outrage to be perpetrated on these helpless creatures."

PATE's means of stopping this outrage is to take photographs of naked supermodels and slap on the caption, "Wouldn't you rather pork me than a pig?"

This follows the pattern of PATE's previous naked supermodel campaigns, like "Spill in me, not in the Gulf," "Don't eat a pig, be one," and, most famously, their anti-hunting poster, "Use your gun on me, big boy."

When interviewed about the knitting circles, one animal rights activist sputters, "I personally know one sheep who was assaulted because no women were available. These damn women. I curse them forever for traumatizing my beautiful sheep friend."

The U.S. Chamber of Commerce also issues a press release. Interestingly enough, when the Chamber of Commerce uses the phrase *press release* it means precisely the same thing AFACASISF does when it uses *rant*. The CoC also eschews the use of the word *communiqué* for essentially the same reason as AFACASISF, in this case because "it is too tainted by its association with liberal communist forces that attempt to inhibit [in this case]

Commercial Freedoms."

The press release states, "The United States Chamber of Commerce is unalterably opposed to the so-called Knitting Circles as they are a barrier to exploitation, and therefore a barrier to commerce. Of course the United States Chamber of Commerce vigorously opposes rape, but even more the USCoC opposes the dangerous mythology that rape is occurring, has ever occurred, could ever occur, or that if it did occur it would be caused by humans. It is the USCoC's unequivocal position that there is no scientific evidence to support the existence of rape. Furthermore, even if rape were to occur, the USCoC holds that it would be good for humans, and far more important, good for the economy.

"The question too few people seem to be asking is this: If these so-called knitting circle groups (which we feel are actually under the influence of professional liberal communist 'outside agitators') are able to stop rape (not that rape exists) then what is to stop these same so-called knitting circle groups and their communist puppet-masters from moving on to stop other forms of so-called exploitation of women, and from there to stopping other forms of so-called exploitation of others? And what if they succeed in stopping all forms of exploitation? What will happen to the economy? It will, of course, collapse. Everyone knows that capitalism is based on and requires systematic exploitation which then magically benefits one and all.

"And finally, the USCoC position is that stopping rape (not that rape occurs) will harm the economy by destroying jobs. We aren't exactly sure how it will do this, but 'saving jobs' is a boilerplate argument we trot out every chance we get, and it's always worked before, so we're trying it again."

Big unions find the jobs argument compelling, for reasons that make no more sense than other times big unions join with big corporations in an attempt to make sure exploitation continues. Especially vocal are various chapters of the United Rapists Union.

Franz Maihem "takes to the street" and interviews URU member Rusty Pike, who says, "I'm proud to be a union rapist, local number 7413. My daddy was a rapist, and his daddy was a rapist, and his daddy before him. We've got rape in our blood. It's an American tradition. Hell, this country was founded on it. The Indians, the land, the women, the workers. Where would this country be without rape? And these women are trying to destroy this proud tradition. They're trying to destroy our lives."

Proclaiming they're tired of not receiving the respect they deserve for doing patriarchy's heavy lifting over the last several thousand years, the United Rapists Union calls a strike, chanting at their rallies, "Hey Hey, Ho Ho, Matriarchy's Got To Go"; and "Rapists, United, Will Always Be Excited." Rusty Pike comments on the strike, "No respect? Well, then, no rape. We'll see how they like that now."

Women like it just fine.

But as with any strike, solidarity becomes an issue. Scabs appear, some on their own, some brought in by various industries with a vested interest in keeping women subservient. This leads to pitched battles between the union rapists and the scab rapists over who exactly has the right to do this necessary work.

In this case, members of various knitting circles do not take sides. Nor, happily, do they take prisoners.

Next to come out against the knitting circles are the United States Departments of Agriculture and Interior, issuing a joint statement that "study after study has shown that it is only through the wise use and management of MVRs (Mobile Vagina Resources) that we can assure that this resource is available to us now and forever. It is noted that the underutilization of MVRs can cause these MVRs to become 'decadent,' or to be wasted. Further, if MVRs were to be severely enough underutilized or were to be managed improperly (as in left on their own) then it is possible this could severely affect future access to the MVRs necessary to keep this nation functioning smoothly. In addition, all use of MVRs (including FUMVRs, or Forcible Use of Mobile Vagina Resources) requires extensive EISs (Environmental Impact Statements) and exhaustive scientific studies, which inevitably show that even FUMVRs have no significant impact on the environment or on human communities. The only exceptions to the requirement of an EIS occurs when the Congress passes categorical exemptions to allow FUMVRs in cases of national emergency or to insure national security by limiting dependence on foreign MVRs, and also to limit the effects of pending Peak MVR. It is further noted, however, that if MVRs do dry up entirely, there do exist suitable if not as desirable substitutes, including NMVRs (Nonhuman Mobile Vagina Resources) and if necessary SIVR(D)s and PIVR(D)s (Silicon and Plastic Immobile Vagina Resources (Detachable) respectively)."

The United States Congress also passes categorical exemptions for both MVRs and FUMVRs as deemed necessary by the Department of Defense, stating that an army fights on and for its MVRs, and that the (probably illegal and certainly immoral) withholding of these MVRs saps a nation's will to fight and constitutes high treason. This exemption is challenged in court, with the United States Supreme Court upholding the exemption by a vote of 11 to 0 (with Clarence Thomas voting three times), citing, then overturning the previous case of *Lysistrata v. Athens.*

Members of knitting circles ignore the USDA, DOI, DOD, the Congress, and the Supremes.

They know what's good for them.

Glenn Beck speaks out against the knitting circles. "I want you to listen carefully, because I'm going to expose some dangerous misconceptions," he says. "Rapes," here he pauses, stares into space. "Rapes do not happen, and when they do happen it is only because women want them to. It's so simple it's complicated, and to help make the complicated simple I'll draw a picture."

He stands, walks to a chalkboard, and draws two dots three feet apart. "The dot on the left is a man. The dot on the right is a woman. He can't be raping her, because he's three feet away. It can't be done, even by someone who is as well endowed as . . . well, we're not here on the Glenn Beck show to talk about Glenn Beck. Anyway, if the male dot wants to rape the female dot, what would it have to do?"

He pauses, looks at the camera.

"Yes, exactly. It would have to *move* toward the female dot." He draws an arrow from the male dot partway toward the female dot. "Now, if this female dot didn't want to be 'raped,' to use their word, what would she do? Exactly, she would move away. And if the man wanted to 'rape' her, to still use their heavily loaded word, the man would have to chase her, to *run*. And the woman would do what? Exactly. She would run away.

"Now, this is the truth no one wants you to know. The

truth so terrifying that only I have the courage and integrity to tell you. The truth is, well, wait—"

He interrupts himself to stare at the camera, compose his face into a thoughtful look, then ask, almost casually, "When was the last time you saw a woman running in terror? Today? Yesterday? The day before? Right now there are plenty of women in this studio, and none of them are running. Sometimes I see women jogging, but, and here's the key point, *no one is chasing them.* These women are running from nothing, and they aren't even running that fast. And even when women do run fast, as at a track meet, still, *no one is chasing them.* So, when women aren't running, no one is raping them, and when women are running, no one is raping them; besides, you couldn't rape someone while she runs! This tells us all we need to know to understand that this 'rape' business is all a fabrication.

"I can hear you thinking, 'But, Glenn, why would these women fabricate such a monstrous plot against innocent men?' I think you know the answer. But I want you to be able to think for yourself and end up thinking just like me, so I'm going to make another diagram."

He erases the dots on the chalkboard and makes a big *X.* He says, "These are two crossed knitting needles. What happens if we break both ends of each knitting needle and turn them ninety degrees, just like these women break truth and turn it ninety degrees?"

He erases each end of the chalk line and redraws it at a perpendicular to reveal: 卐

"These women are socialists! They are lying to us when they say that rape occurs. If they tell us this big lie often enough, we will begin to believe it. Never, ever believe the big lie."

"The Circle of Compassionate Gentleness" posts a blog entry (which is pretty much the only thing they do, except for meditation, yoga, and lots of therapy) stating, "In the softest, kindest, most gentlest terms, the CoCG expresses our most sorrowful, most guilt-inducing, most for-their-own-good disapproval of these heinous acts committed by these misguided women. Yes, we gently and comfortably deplore whatever acts of you-know-what (we prefer never to use the viol--ce word) these women may *perceive* that poor, sad, misguided, wounded men *may* have committed against them, but these poor, sad, misguided, wounded men need our love and compassion and healing. We urge these women, in the softest, kindest, most gentlest terms, to please not upset us by committing heinous acts of viol--ce against these wounded men who can and will be changed by the wonderful power of love and compassion. We would smugly remind these women that gentleness is both a possible and powerful politics, and we would ask them, with glycerin tears in our eyes, to consider the effects and influences of their lives in the light of at least fourteen sacred degrees of separation."

Franz Mayhaim takes time from his busy day cruising porn sites (his favorite is www.mobilevaginaresources.com) to look for love, compassion, and healing on the internet. In fact, that is precisely the phrase he Googles, and up pops the Circle's website. Franz immediately knows he has to interview the Circle's manager and CEO, William McCant.

They meet at the Circle's offices, offices so gentle they have no sharp corners that could be hurty and no doors that could obstruct the movement of compassion.

Franz asks, "So, William, presuming that rape actually

exists, something about which the science is extremely clouded, what are the most important things we can do to stop rape?"

McCant answers, smoothly, gently, "First, stop trying to stop rape. This sounds counterintuitive, but it's based on several profound manifestations of my own wise understanding. The first is that it's not our job to stop rape or to save women. Women don't need us to save them. Women don't even need to save themselves. To say they need to be saved implies that the eternal now is not already eternally perfect, and to do so is to insult the power of living and experiencing what we are living and experiencing right now. It is to ignore the power of the now. The now is incredibly powerful, Franz. You are here, and I am here. And there is no rape taking place right here, Franz. Do you see how powerful and transformative this is? The question isn't, 'How can I stop rape?' but rather, it's 'How can I become more present here? How can I learn to listen better to what's going on for me, within me, around me? Why are these women so unenlightened and so impatient and so demanding that they presume the present isn't good enough, when that's all they have to work with? Why do they presume the present isn't good enough simply because they are being sexually assaulted? Franz, these women need to do some serious work on themselves."

"You're right, William, that's very profound."

"Thank you. I prefer to be called Willie."

"Got it, Willie."

"Second, trying to save anybody or anything often ends up with well-intentioned blindness. People become so convinced they're on the Side of The Angels that they don't think to question themselves. That, then, all too easily leads to shoulds, musts, and have-tos, directed at other people. It becomes so easy then to blame rapists for their actions, to say that they 'should not' rape, they 'must not' rape, they 'have to' not rape. And that sort of well-intentioned arrogance is a blight that must be eliminated through whatever passive-aggressive means we can muster. Third, I find it a little disheartening to have expectations or aspirations so huge they approach the infinitudes of impossibility, when I think of little ol' me in my little ol' life. I avoid despair where I can, because it is hurty, and it makes me feel so sad, and I don't want to feel sad, because feeling sad makes me sad." Willie stops a moment, sucks his thumb. When he's able to continue, he says, "Stopping rape sounds like something for a superhero, and the last time I checked, I'm no superhero. But to keep myself from feeling as completely ineffective as I really am, I have to assume at every moment that I do make a difference, somehow, even when it's clear I don't. So, since I'm not really a stop rape kind of guy, and since I don't want to feel bad about not being a stop rape kind of guy, it's important to me that no one else try to stop rape, or it will make me feel inferior, like I should actually be doing something instead of sitting on my beautifully gentle buttocks in my beautifully gentle office, beautifully and gently meditating. So I think the women should stop trying to stop rape. That is the first step toward stopping rape."

Franz says, "That is brilliant, and brilliantly compassionate, Willie."

Willie McCant says, "Thank you, and I prefer to be called Li'l Willie."

"Understood, Li'l Willie."

Li'l Willie continues, "We have to place our small changes in a larger context, to discover the ways the insignificant changes we make in our own lives link to larger currents, structures, movements, resonances, vibes. We have to look at chaos theory, quantum theory, string theory, all these scientific theories that I don't understand but that nonetheless show me how me sitting here and delighting in the sensation of the heat emanating into my buttocks from this electrically heated ergonomic meditation pillow will help suffering people everywhere. I am sending this comfort and pleasure into the world, and just as in capitalism a rising tide lifts all boats, so my own happiness and comfort raises the universal happiness and comfort quotient for the world, lifting everyone else's happiness and comfort. So when I hear of some atrocity somewhere, I know the best thing I can do is make myself more happy and comfortable, because I know the happier and more comfortable I am, the happier everyone, including the victims of those atrocities, will be. It's scientific!"

Franz is barely able to articulate, "I'm in awe, Li'l Willie. Absolutely stunned."

Li'l Willie says, "Thank you, Franz. I prefer to be called Tiger."

Franz murmurs, "I can see why."

Tiger continues, "It is this knowledge that allows me to face up to even a tiny fraction of the horrors out there: the knowledge that each time I perceive some horror, my role in fighting back—and I'm a very big part of the struggle—is to make myself more and more comfortable and happy. Because we can't avoid all knowledge of these atrocities. If I could avoid that knowledge, I would, since that knowledge is so hurty. But I can't. Clear-cutting happens. Mountaintop removal mining happens. 'Ethnic cleansing' happens. Corporate greed happens. War happens. 'Rape' happens."

Franz interjects, "Or it may not. There is serious doubt among some scientists."

"That's why I put quote marks around the word *rape*, Franz.

But the important thing is not whether or not it does happen. The important thing is that we not assign responsibility in any case. I said, 'Rape happens.' I did not say that anyone commits any of these atrocities, because I want to stay away from any notion of blame. I want to stay away from any notion of blame because if we assign responsibility, 'He raped her,' or 'He ordered a clear-cut,' then we are back in the land of judgment, implying he should not rape her; he should not order that clear-cut. And we can't make those judgments, because having made those judgments it becomes morally reprehensible not to take the sides of the victims, and having taken the side of the victim it becomes morally reprehensible to not act decisively to defend that victim. And I'm not a stop-rape kind of guy, so I need to not start down that path at all, but rather become extremely adept at the use of passive voice."

There follows the sort of comfortable silence that passes between the insufferably smug when they're drawn together by common desires and techniques to avoid taking responsibility.

Finally Franz says, "Brilliant, Tiger. Nothing less."

Tiger says, "Thank you. I prefer to be called Li'l Willie, Tiger Boy."

Franz says, "Your wish is my command."

Li'l Willie, Tiger Boy, says, "Rowr."

Franz smiles, his whole body tingling.

Li'l Willie, Tiger Boy, says, "The most important thing about any conversation is that it end by being about me. So when you ask what are the most important things we can do to stop rape, I immediately ask, 'How can I clarify what is most important to me?' I think it's important to regularly check in with myself about what's important to me. In fact it's so important I'm going to say that it's important to regularly check in with myself about what's important to me again and again. And it's important for me to check in with others too to make sure they know what's important to me. So, when you ask me what are the most important things we can do to stop rape, I ask the same 'question cycle' I ask about everything: 1) What's important to me? 2) What's important to others? 3) What about what's important to me comes from others, other times, or other places? 4) What would I like to be important to me?"

Franz says, "I'm confused, Li'l Willie, Tiger Boy. I thought we were talking about rape (presuming it occurs)."

Li'l Willie, Tiger Boy, responds, "I thought we were talking about me. But if you do want to talk about rape (presuming it occurs), here are some suggestions I would make to the knitting circle women. I don't think they are very courageous. I think they're taking the easy way out, the harmful way out. It doesn't take any courage to use a knitting needle to stab a man who has two guns, three knives, a chain, and steel-toed boots, a man who outweighs you by a hundred pounds, and who is because of his own prior woundings attempting to do you great bodily harm. That takes no courage whatsoever. I'll tell you what takes courage—and it takes courage right now for me to sit on my electrically heated ergonomic meditation pillow and say this to you, because I don't think you'll take my advice, I think you'll reject me, I think you'll act without consideration for my feelings whatsoever, and you won't even care if you are hurty and you make me cry, but I'm going to tell you anyway. It takes courage to remain small and ineffectual. I challenge these women to have the courage to *be*, to be present in the perfect and eternal now. I challenge them to have the courage to learn, the courage to learn what it was in their past lives or in their past energy that has called this into their lives, the courage to learn the wondrous lesson life is trying to teach them by giving them this wonderful opportunity, the courage to open themselves up to others, physically, emotionally, spiritually, including to those they may *perceive* as exploiting them, the courage to see things from the so-called rapists' perspective (as I do), and to ask themselves why they so desperately want to hurt these poor innocent wounded men whose only crime is that they need love and acceptance and don't know how to get it. And finally, I would urge them to have the courage to see things from my perspective, to see that their actually fighting back makes me feel ashamed of my own cowardice."

"Thank you, Li'l Willie, Tiger Boy. Any final thoughts?"

"Yes, thank you, although I prefer to be called by my full name, William McCant. I do have a beautiful, powerful story to end with. Many centuries ago a devout Buddhist woman was walking along a forest path. She was ambushed by bandits, who raped her . . ."

"So there actually is evidence of rape existing?"

"We only have her word for it, which probably isn't worth much, but on with the story. Instead of resisting, she allowed herself to be raped by the bandits with such grace and compassion that the bandits converted to Buddhism on the spot, as soon as they were finished."

Franz says, "That's an extraordinarily powerful story, William McCant. It's so, like, spiritual and deep. And I can see how this story will make things so much easier for so many of us." He turns toward the camera. "Did you hear this story, Katherine? Tonight, baby, I challenge you to convert me to Buddhism!"

But suddenly Franz's vacuous smile disappears. He stops moving. He is troubled by a thought, for two reasons. The first is that he's never actually had one before, which means that having an original thought is very uncomfortable in and of itself. He wonders for a moment if this is what brain cancer feels like. And he's also troubled because the thought itself is troubling. He says, "But if the enlightened thing to do is to let perpetrators perpetrate, and to do so with compassion, and doing this is supposed to help them stop perpetrating, doesn't that mean we should let the knitting circle murderers continue their murders, and if we do so with compassion in our hearts this will convert these women to being pacifists?"

William McCant pulls his pacifier out of his pocket, and sucks on it. He closes his eyes. Finally he opens his eyes, uses his right hand to tenderly take the pacifier from his mouth (keeping it close for quick reinsertion if necessary), and says, "I thought you were going to ask a question, but you never said anything."

So Franz repeats the question.

This time William sucks on the pacifier while holding his hands over his ears and humming "Amazing Grace."

Franz waits.

By fits and starts William McCant stops humming. He opens one eye, then the other. He says, "You're still here."

Having never before come up with a meaningful question, Franz is willing to give it one more try. He asks again.

This time William McCant doesn't pitch a fit. He simply answers, "Oh, no. These women aren't reachable. They won't stop. They should all be strung up. But gently and with compassion."

CHAPTER 9

With the knitting craze swelling into a national obsession, and with rapists disappearing faster than capitalists in an ethics contest, federal lawmakers step in.

Senator Richard Dick, square-jawed, bullet-headed, dead-eyed, and with a smile only a lobbyist could love, delivers a speech which concludes, "We must ban knitting needles immediately. We have never faced criminal terrorists as vicious as these lunatics who want to destroy our precious freedom and democracy."

Senator Hassemann, the Senator voted least likely to be allowed to have children sit on his lap as well as the Senator most likely to violate his multiple restraining orders, continues, ". . . and our fun. You don't go far enough by half, Senator Dick. It's not surprising that you're soft on terrorism. We must also ban crochet hooks, plus all wool, cotton, and even acrylic yarns. We must immediately initiate sheep eradication programs, even though that is bound to affect my social life. Starve these illegal enemy combatants of the means to commit their terrorist atrocities."

Senator Eve Pankhurst, who was appointed to her position after the death of her predecessor, and who knows the lobbyists will vote her out as soon as they can, says, "Those who would choose security over sweaters deserve neither. Knitting has been a fundamental right since the beginning of this nation, a proud tradition begun by our foremothers. And furthermore, if we outlaw knitting needles, only outlaws will have knitting needles.

Every woman in this building opposes this ban."

The acting head of the Senate, who looks like he's been dead for several hundred years, says, "Since we're unanimous, we don't need any debate. The ban passes."

Debate does, however, break out in every corner of every city and town across the country. Everyone takes sides, and not always the sides you'd think.

Picture this: Dozens of people, many wearing camouflage, all carrying guns and knitting needles, sit on folding chairs in a room lined with wood paneling, stuffed animal heads (including a couple of children's plush toy stuffed animal heads among the deer and elk), and a big NRA logo. They are listening to a speech. The speaker, wearing a Bullwinkle the Moose hat, waves his fist and shouts, "Today they take our knitting needles, tomorrow our rocket propelled grenades. We must oppose this creeping fascism!"

At a meeting across town, a tall, slender man stands at a lectern wearing a suit and a tie. He holds a copy of the constitution, and copies of books by both William F. Buckley and Noam Chomsky, to let the audience know he's well read, an "intellectual," and "open-minded." Underneath his unbuttoned suit coat he wears a Heinz 57 T-shirt to make sure the audience also knows he's a "regular guy" who knows how to "chill out" and "have fun." His audience consists of four bibliophiles, two homeless people coming in out of the rain, a couple of teenagers in the back making out, and radio and television crews from NPR and C-Span respectively. He pontificates to the mostly empty chairs, "I see nothing in the constitution that guarantees the right to bear knitting needles. Bear arms, yes. Bear children, of course! But not knitting needles."

One of the homeless people raises her hand and mumbles something.

The speaker points to her. "You have a question! Madam, please speak up!"

She asks, "Why does he get a pitcher of water, and I don't? I demand my rights!"

Or picture this: a paved road travels to the horizon between fields of tasseled corn. Old skid marks weave across faded asphalt. A dotted yellow line travels till it disappears in heat waves. A Ford Fiesta zooms by so fast you can barely make out the paired bumper stickers on the back: "Jesus Saves" and "Knitting Needles Still a Beating Heart."

Soon after, an ancient Dodge pickup chugs by, this with a single sticker on its bumper: "You can have my knitting needles when you pry them from my cold, dead fingers." It passes slowly enough for you to spot a small blue-haired head barely higher than the steering wheel, and a knitting needle rack in the pickup's rear window.

Or picture this: it's Oscar Night, and elegance prevails, from the red carpets to the overdramatic music to all the stars decked out in their really fucking expensive designer outfits. The camera pans across a row, revealing to the millions of television viewers their heroes (heroes, celebrities—you say tomato, I say tomahto): Susan Sarandon, Barbra Streisand, Tom Hanks, Matt Damon, and Tim Robbins all wearing small wool strings pinned to their lapels with tiny (solid 24-karat) gold knitting needles.

As happens so often in governmental Wars on Inanimate Objects, the government's War on Yarn leads to some unintended consequences and unforeseen circumstances.

Two customs officers at the Oakland docks—brothers

named Herman and Melvin—don't work quite so hard as the other officers. They mainly spend their time coauthoring what they hope will be The Great American Novel. It's about a mad whale who relentlessly pursues a one-legged sea captain. Their first draft had been about a one-legged whale who relentlessly pursues a mad sea captain, until they realized the obvious problem: how do you tell a mad sea captain from one who is sane? The novel begins, "'Call me Ishmael,' he wailed." That's pretty much as far as they've gotten.

Nonetheless, they are madly scribbling notes when one of their field officers, a bright young woman named Delly, brings in her list of U.S. inbound manifests on the allotment of containers the three are supposed to inspect. The brothers don't look up from their scribbling as they say, in unison, "Begin."

She does, reading aloud page after page describing imported junk. They never stop scribbling.

She gets to the last page. "Here we have a container of TNT being sent to 'Domestic Terrorism, Inc.,' in Rexburg, Idaho."

They keep scribbling.

"A load of anthrax ampoules, being sent to 'White American Heroes!' otherwise known as WAH!'"

They keep scribbling.

"One full container of heroin, 99 percent pure, being sent from a 'Mr. Big' to some certain offices in Langley, Virginia."

Herman waves his hand dismissively.

"Two containers labeled 'fissionable materials' sent from Al Qaeda Central to the local Al Qaeda franchise in Boger City, North Carolina."

Melvin asks, "Why are you wasting our time with this stuff? Anything else?"

Delly takes a deep breath, then says as quickly and quietly

as she can, almost mumbling, "One more. A shipment of yarn and needles from—"

Herman and Melvin simultaneously leap to their feet, and cry, "Confiscate that container. Alert Homeland Security!"

In the Mexican desert, near the border with Arizona, two hippies stand next to a car. One of them is holding a bunch of knitting needles. He says, "Well, what do you do when you smuggle weed, man?"

The other responds, "I put it in the tires, dude. They never check there."

An hour later their car crawls along the road with four flat tires, knitting needles piercing the rubber. "Bummer, man."

A man wearing a long coat and loitering in Washington Square Park in New York City hisses softly, "Spikes, string, I got it all, man."

In a basement in Arcata, California, 1000 watt grow lamps blaze over a "scene" of cotton plants. Upstairs, a woman spins yarn. She proudly tells her friend, "This strain is called White Widow."

A man is being hauled across his front yard by a pair of police officers. A bashful yet beautiful sheep peeks out his front door. The man pleads, "But it was only for personal use!"

Hollywood knows a good thing when it sees it. It doesn't take long for American remake of *The Girl with the Knitted Dragon Sweater* to hit the big screen. The movie stars Daniel Craig as Nick, and—well, it doesn't really matter who the women in the film are, so long as they have big breasts. The codirectors, Lars von Trier and David Fincher, both deeply troubled by what they perceive as the muddled message of this movement—

"Stop Rape or Face the Wrath of the Knitting Circle"—decide to clarify their message by putting out a series of promotional posters for the film that feature various actors—since they are women, their names don't really matter, do they?—nude, with the posters trailing into suggestive darkness a couple of inches below the women's navels. In these posters Daniel Craig stands fully clothed, one arm protectively around a woman's torso (but not, of course, covering her breasts), and the other brandishing a knitting needle.

When women complain that these posters demean women, Lars von Trier issues a press release declaring that he will not pander to the whims or demands of any minority group, even one that constitutes an actual majority of human beings. Further, he states, there's no way he could sell the movie to his target audience of males between the ages of eighteen and thirty-five "without showing some major boobage." He concludes his press release with the questions, "How could these posters demean women? I mean, for God's sake, they show beautiful young women with beautiful young tits. What more could anyone want?"

When women complain that so often in films, "the women get younger and younger and nuder and nuder," von Trier responds, "That's all I needed to hear. I most definitely intend for the women in this film to get younger and younger and nuder and nuder."

When the film is finally released, viewers learn that, in order to make the film "more psychologically complex and, you know, edgy," to use von Trier's words, the women do not use the knitting needles to kill rapists, but rather, in what von Trier openly declares is an homage to "the greatest filmmaker of all time, Lars von Trier," they use the knitting needles to reproduce a scene from one of his earlier films and mutilate their own genitals.

Members of the knitting circle know, however, that there are much better places to put their needles.

Suzie and Jasmine go for a walk in the park, stepping over goose poop on their way to the lake.

Suzie says, "I'm very concerned about your boyfriend."

"Why?"

"I don't know how to ask this," Suzie says, "but is he for real?"

"Oh, yes, this all feels so right to me! So real!"

"No, I mean, does he really exist?"

"Exist?"

"Like you or me."

Jasmine giggles, says, "Well, he's got some differences . . ."

"Like . . ."

"I'm not going to talk about that!"

"Here's what I'm trying to ask: have you met him except for those times you said at the Xanadu?"

"Yes! We meet all the time! Almost every night!"

"You do? You haven't told me about that. What's he like?"

"Like I said at Grandma Ahn's, he's really changeable."

"That's what I didn't understand. Do you mean, like he's inconsistent? One day nice, the next day angry? That's not a good sign, Jaz."

"No, I meant what I said at the nursing home. It's his looks. It's so wonderful. One night I'm hanging out with Brad Pitt, and then a wombat, and lately a centaur. Centaurs are the sexiest!"

"Jaz, I'm getting very worried about you."

"And sometimes when he comes up to me hearts burst into

the room and fly away like little red butterflies!"

"Jaz?"

"You ask, is he real? It doesn't get any more real than The One, does it?"

Billy Bob walks down the stairs to the MAWAR office, partly because he never can get quite enough peeks at the August cheesecake from the defunct tire company calendar, and partly because he suspects Zebadiah is on the computer again, and presumably up to no good.

He's not so worried that Zebadiah might be looking at porn. No one in MAWAR has ever been interested in anything more than cheesecake, and they've not even been interested enough in that to update their calendar. For some reason their leader always seems more interested in updating the Twelve Monthly Miracles of Jesus calendars. Besides, someone once installed a porn alarm on the computer that would go off anytime anyone typed in a search that matched potential porn triggers, and in the whole year's subscription the only times it went off were false positives, as when someone searched for phrases like the Virgin Mary, inflamed prostate (first having looked up enflamed prostate, which would have been an entirely different health problem), Onan (embarrassingly enough), or David and Bathsheba, this latter because the porn alarm considered the scene where David sees Bathsheba bathing on the rooftop too racy.

But he still wants to know what he's doing on the computer.

Billy Bob peeks around the corner to see Zebadiah staring at the screen. Zebadiah sees him, too, and quickly taps a few times at the keyboard.

Billy Bob asks, "What lookest thou at on the computer?"

"Nothing."

"Let me see."

Zebadiah shows him.

Billy Bob says, "That's just the username and password page. That doesn't do me any good."

Zebadiah says, "That's the point." He gets up and leaves.

But Billy Bob has watched enough detective movies on television to know that most people's usernames and passwords can be discovered in mere moments—and certainly before the next commercial—if chance will merely provide the right clues to set off a brilliant series of semilogical leaps on the part of the detective. So, he looks around the room, sees the cheesecake, and types in "tires" and "round" (since that's what tires are). Nothing. He sees the picture of Jesus and types in "Jesus" and "OurLordandSavior" but that doesn't work either. He starts to think the detective shows might not be as accurate as he had hoped.

But he gets the same lucky break they always get in the mystery movies when Zebadiah turns on the stereo upstairs and starts to blast *Ted Nugent Plays Gospel Favorites*. Billy Bob listens to the first song—"How Great Thou Art"—thinks about Zebadiah's taste in music, types in "wretched" for a username, realizes that Zebadiah would of course not say that about his own musical tastes, deletes that word, and types in "HowGreatTedArt." He feels comfortable with this. But he still needs a password. He closes his eyes, lets his mind drift. He thinks about Jezebel/Jasmine, about the courage Zebadiah has to even consider getting so close to such an agent of Beelzebub. He thinks how Zebadiah must have . . . That's it! He types in "holyfuckingnadsofsteel" and hits enter.

He is shocked by what comes up on the screen. He knows that he and Zebadiah need to talk, and they need to talk now.

It takes a surprisingly short time for Zebadiah to move through Elisabeth Kübler-Ross's stages of "having been caught doing something stupid," zooming past defensiveness, blaming someone else, embarrassment, and humiliation right to enthusiasm and pride and "it's really cool and everybody else is doing it anyway."

Billy Bob says, "Okay, let me get this straight. You pay real money so you can have a second 'life' on a computer?"

"Well, I figured since I don't have a life in reality, I may as well have one somewhere, and besides, it's only ten dollars a month! That's not too much to pay to have a life, is it?"

"Brother Zebadiah—"

"And it's even better. I own land there!"

"Own land, on the computer?"

"And you should see how much land I own! Look!" A few clicks and Zebadiah is showing Billy Bob his mansion, complete with 3-D moving pictures of Jesus on every wall, and even on the floor, with the floor Jesuses always deftly stepping out of the way of the user's virtual foot.

Despite himself, Billy Bob is impressed. "You've got yourself a nice piece of property, Brother Zebadiah."

"And it only costs me another hundred dollars a month."

"Wait. You pay real money for a fake house?"

"At thirty-five dollars per plasma donation, and at two donations per week, I can pay for my monthly rental in only ten days. That leaves me with all the other donations to use for spending money. How do you think I bought the 'water into wine' fountain for the grand entry hall?"

"You trade blood for pixels?"

"Yes, but everybody's doing it, aren't they? Isn't that what the whole computer culture is about, trading real life for virtual life? I'm on the leading edge, Billy Bob! I'm on the front lines of yet another revolution."

Billy Bob nods grimly. "Thou doest surely have holy fucking nads of steel. But isn't this blood donation all too much? Doth it not make thee really fucking weak?"

"Well, I've also been selling to the sperm bank."

"Selling to the sperm bank? Unfaithful to Jezebel already?"

"Jasmine!"

"Have you told her?"

"No. It's just that sometimes when we are chatting on here . . ."

"You meet her in this computer place?"

"Yes, and sometimes when we are chatting here and I start thinking about her that way, I just tell her I have to go to work."

Billy Bob thinks a moment. "How much doth thou make for these holy donations?"

"One hundred dollars, Brother Billy Bob."

"One hundred dollars a whack?"

"It is good money, my brother. Thou shouldst try it."

"But I still do not understand. Good money to buy a house in computerville? A house that doth not really exist?"

"It may not exist, Billy Bob, but like you saw, it's really big." Zebadiah shows him more of his property, including the swimming pool. He says, "The pool has an adjustable temperature, so when it's cold in computerville I make it an Olympic-size hot tub, and when it's warm I turn the pool way down. It feels so good!"

"Feels?"

"And look what else my character can do!" Zebadiah pushes a button and suddenly hearts flutter all over the screen and flit away like butterflies. He says, "So whenever I see Jasmine

I can shower her with hearts!" He says, proudly, "I paid $200 for that ability."

Billy Bob's eyes go wide.

Zebadiah says, "That's only one whack and three pints of blood . . . and it sure is pretty!"

Billy Bob tells their leader, who calls a MAWAR meeting. There it is determined that while they all appreciate Zebadiah's creativity in moving to ensnare the heathen Jezebel through getting to know her on a computer, he must in fact call her, and he must in fact see her in real life, no matter how scary this may be for him. They urge him to remember that Jesus and his guardian angels will be with him at every moment, and that while he may sometimes walk afraid, he will never walk alone. He strenuously argues against all of this, saying that his plan only needs more time, and that he has already been saving up for a gilded prison room for her in computerville, and it would only have taken another couple of months of blood and masturbation before it would be ready. They point out to him that kidnapping her in computerville would not actually serve their purpose. They need to kidnap her in real life. It takes a while to convince him of this distinction.

At this point it is clear that Zebadiah is not only frightened, but that his pride is hurt over the failure of his other plan. To mollify him, all members of MAWAR agree that from this time forward, they will never again call her Jezebel, and that when they play Bible Scrabble the word *Jezebel* will be worth only half points. These concessions make Zebadiah happy, and help him gird his loins to move forward.

Suzie and Sam are once again in bed. They are, sadly, once again fully clothed. Suzie says to Sam, "Now do you believe that even taking into account the brainwashing and training of our oppressive patriarchal culture, I genuinely want to make love with you?"

Sam responds, "I sort of believe it. I think we could proceed, as long as we're careful. I think that not only should we be absolutely certain that in advance, in the abstract, that we want to make love, but that at each step of the way, in the concrete, we agree with each action, and verbally acknowledge that we still indeed want it."

Suzie says, reasonably enough, "Huh?"

Sam says, "I'll show you. Can I kiss your lips?"

"Oh god yes, I've only been begging you to start!" She grabs him and pulls him on top of her, and kisses him passionately.

He backs off hurriedly. "No, no. You're missing my point. We should each ask consent about every part. Like this: Can I touch your arm?"

"Are you kidding me?"

"See? You don't want me to. It's a good thing I asked."

"No, I mean, really, you're going to ask each time you touch a new body part?"

"It's the only way I can be sure that you want me to do it. And to be fair, you should ask me as well."

Suzie sighs. "Okay. I want you to feel comfortable. Can I touch your shoulder?"

"I'd love that. Can I touch your hair?"

"Absolutely. Can I kiss your neck?"

"Mmm."

"Is that a 'yes'?"

"Yes!"

"Just making sure. Can I touch your chest?"

"Not yet," Sam says. "Go a bit slower, please. Can I kiss your fingers?"

"Go for it. Can I run the fingers of my other hand down the inside of your arm?"

"Yes, that would feel good."

Their voices fade. Romantic music swells. They caress each other slower and slower, asking about each individual touch and not getting very far before they both fall asleep. They both snore softly, as cute as kittens.

Weeks pass, and we are back at MAWAR headquarters, where the NASCAR Jesuses continue to serenely overlook the three ugliest lamps on the planet.

The leader says, "The fuckin' cops won't do their job to stop these devils. The feds aren't doing it. And the commie pinko liberal media certainly doesn't give a rat's ass. It's up to us to do the righteous work of the Lord and smite the wicked."

The group responds as one, "Amen!"

Their leader says, "Brother Zebadiah! It's been weeks since we made our new arrangement. The situation is deteriorating. Why hast thou not yet nabbed Jasmine? I thought you were on the cusp of glory!"

Zebadiah responds, "I'm almost there! All praise to the Lord!"

Their leader says, "Then why hast thou not brought that hussy home!"

Zebadiah says, "You said you'd call her Jasmine!"

"I said I'd not call her Jezebel, and I didn't call her that name."

"You're cheating."

"Don't change the subject, Brother Zebadiah. You've been out with her three times! Do you even have a single testicle? We need her so we can bargain with the heathens!"

Zebadiah says, earnestly, "I couldn't take her home on the first date. Even for Jesus. It would have been too great a sin."

Billy Bob asks, "What about the second date? I'm sure you would have been forgiven for that."

Zebadiah says, "Just thinking about it made me feel impure. On our third date, I tried to pray for her soul, but Jasmine made disparaging remarks about Our Lord. I couldn't countenance that."

Billy Bob says, "You don't have to like that demon spawn. Just. Bring. Her. Home."

Zebadiah responds, "I've been praying my ass off over this, Brother. I believe the Lord wanted me to wait. Bringing a woman home on the fourth date is only a minor sin. So I made another date with her for Friday. I'm ready for the glory!"

Their leader says, "Lemme hear an Amen!"

The room explodes with a hearty Amen.

Their leader says, "It's do-or-die time, Brother Zebadiah. Make the Lord proud. Be strong in righteous ass-kickery! We are the last best hope for godly men! Go forth with the fire of the Lord's fury burning in your loins!"

The men in the room respond with an Amen that leaves the NASCAR Jesuses rocking back and forth in its wake.

Jasmine and Suzie are back the Red Moon Sacred Gyn Mill Tea House for Wimmin of All Kinds and Kindreds, eating the only edible item on the menu. Jasmine fills in Suzie on her recent dates with Zebadiah.

Suzie says, "He pretended to pray for your soul?"

Jasmine responds, "I thought it was tasteless, you know? Making fun of Christian fundamentalists like that. I told him it was tacky, like mocking the mentally ill. Because isn't that really what he was doing?"

"So, Jaz, why are you going out with him again?"

"I admit he's a little weird. And I'm not so sure any more that he's The One. But he's cute, and maybe I could convince myself that his freaky quirks are charming eccentricities. Right?"

"I don't know if I could do that. He seems kind of repulsive."

"Yeah. But I'm not sure he's quite bad enough for me to not date him. It's easy for you to judge—you've got Sam. It's different for me. I'm almost twenty-three years old, and even before Zebadiah I hadn't had a boyfriend for a whole three months! I don't want to wind up sixty-two years old, alone on the streets, a ranting bag lady."

Suzie thinks, then comments, "Getting married is no guarantee you won't end up alone, a ranting bag lady in the streets. It can happen to anyone."

Jasmine sighs. "I know. I know. If he keeps being weird, I'll stop seeing him. But I want to give our relationship one more chance. I can't give up yet. I've invested too many daydreaming hours figuring out the color scheme of our wedding."

Nick hasn't left Brigitte's for months. She doesn't have an attic, so he hasn't been able to hide there. Nor has he kept his promise to not make a peep. Mainly he's sat in front of the television, obsessively watching news of the knitting needle phenomenon and getting on Brigitte's nerves, as she has gotten on his. But the "nonrelationship" has survived as well as could have been hoped.

As Franz and Chet chatter ominously on the TV, Brigitte picks up her tote bag and car keys. She says, "I'm going out, Nick. Do you want anything?"

"Where are you going?" Nick asks.

Brigitte responds, slightly annoyed, "Various errands."

"When will you be back?" he asks.

"Nick, I know you're stir-crazy, stuck in my home as a fugitive. But let's not forget who we are, okay? We're very independent people. We like that about each other. If you start asking me where I'm going and when I'll be back every time I go anywhere, it's going to depress me more than I already am with you here. I'm starting to feel like you're my mother, or worse, my husband."

He says, "I'm sorry. I know. I can't seem to help myself."

She responds, "It sneaks up on people when they live together."

"I never wanted this to happen. We're becoming just like cranky, boring married people, with lives stripped of charm and mystery. Bleh. I don't want us to lose the magic, Brigitte. I want the romance, the hot lust, the fun."

She says, "Let's try this again. I'm going out—do you want anything?"

"Yes. We're out of cookies and I'm desperate. The round ones with the flaky dough and the strawberry filling? About this big?"

"I know the ones."

They smile and she goes out the door. He turns back to the TV.

The president addresses the nation in a press conference. He says, "We urge patience, vigilance, and calm. I assure you, the American people, that the Knitting Needle Killings are nearly under control and will be stopped."

The president's wife, standing behind him, starts laughing maniacally. The press roars with questions. Two big men with wires coiling out of their ears appear and rush the president's wife off stage.

The president continues, "Ahem. In fact, I am honored to announce that we have a new ally and partner to work with us to fight this war on terror. Al Qaeda has pledged to dedicate the full force of its organization in this effort."

The promises (or threats) of the President of the United States notwithstanding, the knitting circle movement has now gone beyond stopping rape. The movement wants to go all the way to liberate women. Now that women have gotten a taste of their own power, the uprising has become unstoppable. It spreads all over the world.

It's time for a montage! To your favorite feminist revolutionary internationalist anthem!

In massive protests and riots, women overturn armored trucks containing yarn and needles. Women battle police, dodge tear gas and rubber bullets, and then real bullets. They fire back. Women blow up malls, fast food restaurants, and chain stores, including stores selling women's fashion. *Especially* stores selling women's fashion.

In Japan, women wearing knitted Hello Kitty hats chase men in western business suits.

In an airport in Thailand, women and children wield needles as German businessmen flee.

In Afghanistan, women in knitted burkas chase bearded men and foreign soldiers amid the rubble.

In the Near East, Israeli and Palestinian women chase Israeli settlers and soldiers, and Palestinian men.

In Africa, women chase men down a dusty street.

The same scenes unfold in Latin America and Europe.

In Antarctica, three female scientists chase three male scientists through a field of penguins.

A woman wearing a knitted space suit cover floats outside the space shuttle and aims a needle at a man who is also outside the space shuttle. He floats away, leaking precious air, never to corner her in the cockpit again.

But there remains one final threat to the liberation movement.

CHAPTER 10

Zebadiah and Jasmine stand outside the MAWAR headquarters. It looks like a normal dumpy house in a normal dumpy neighborhood. He uses a key to unlock the door. Meanwhile, Jasmine plans the improvements she would make—fresh paint, a few flowers—in the event she and Zeb get married one day.

Zebadiah says to Jasmine, "I'm kind of tired of talking about me . . ."

She looks at him, anticipating at long last a question—any sort of question—about her life.

He continues, "Why don't *you* talk about me for a while?"

He turns on the lights. Jasmine moves into the living room. He closes and locks the door, then flicks shut nine more deadbolts. Jasmine hears the clicks and looks back at him, slightly troubled. He ignores her and walks into the kitchen. She hears him rummaging around. She sits in a chair, notices the lamps. These are even more troubling than the locks.

Zebadiah returns from the kitchen holding rope and duct tape.

Jasmine frowns. "I'm not into that."

The four other MAWAR men come out of a bedroom, wearing their MAWAR shirts.

Jasmine's eyes widen. She says, "I'm definitely not into that."

MAWAR's leader points at her. "You may not be into God, but God is definitely into you."

A few minutes later, Jasmine is tied to a chair, with duct tape over her mouth.

The leader says, "Thank you, Brother Zebadiah, for your holy contribution to our glorious mission. Good work!"

Billy Bob turns to face Jasmine. "You, missy, have become a lucky pawn in the great chess game of the Lord."

Jasmine looks puzzled.

Billy Bob points to his T-shirt logo. "We are MAWAR: Men Against Women Against Rape."

Jasmine's eyes widen in terror, and she attempts a strangled scream.

Billy Bob continues, "Chill out, sinner. We're not rapists. We're men of God defending the Holy Law as it is written."

Jasmine looks puzzled.

Billy Bob says, "Where in the Ten Holy Fucking Commandments does it ever say, 'Thou Shalt Not Rape'? Huh? The answer is, it doesn't. In fact, the whole fuckin' Bible is filled with rapes that fulfill God's merciful will. We will not tolerate heresy from a bunch of stupid demons . . . infidels . . . heathens . . . women."

Jasmine rolls her eyes in disbelief.

Billy Bob rips the tape from Jasmine's mouth. He says, "You're going to call off your people."

She spits, "Or what are you going to do?"

Billy Bob looks meaningfully into the kitchen.

Suzie and Sam are in her bedroom, still, pathetically enough, fully dressed. The phone rings. Suzie answers it.

She hears Jasmine's voice, yelling, in tears and with terror, "They're going to force me to make pies for the church bake sale!"

Hours later, Suzie paces, distraught, while Sam stares at the wall, angry and determined, distractedly hitting a pillow over and over.

Suzie says, "We have to get her out of there. They're making her bake? Soon she'll be scrubbing and ironing. It will not stop!"

Sam continues to stare. Then he looks at Suzie. Suzie can see in his eyes the beginning of an idea. At last he says to her, "Let me go in. I can take these guys on. I shall challenge them to a duel!"

The next day, the members of MAWAR are gathered at headquarters. Their leader says, "That asshole challenged us to a what?"

Billy Bob answers, "A duel."

Their leader: "A duel?"

Billy Bob: "A motherfuckin' duel."

Their leader: "Fuck. We can't get out of that."

Zebadiah asks, "Why not?"

Billy Bob answers him, "The whole honor thing. Some asshole challenges you to a duel, you don't refuse unless you're a fuckin' pussy."

Zebadiah says, "Oh yeah. The honor thing."

They silently ruminate on honor for a few moments, before their leader says, "Which of us is going to take on this motherfucker? Which of us has the balls to kick some heathen profeminist ass for Christ?"

"There's really only one choice," says Billy Bob.

Everyone looks at the biggest, baddest guy in the room.

Ezekiel stands up. He's a mountain of muscled flesh. He smiles and cracks his knuckles.

Picture an old gym. A really old gym. An extremely old gym. No, not quite as old as the one you're imagining, but about three-quarters of the way there. The bricks on the walls are chipped and decaying. They're stained by decades of sweat and cigar smoke and the broken dreams of broken men. At one time the room may have been brightly lit, but time, incompetence, and an unwillingness to pay for a good union electrician have combined to render half of the overhead lights useless. Or maybe it's just that the bulbs need to be replaced. In any case, the place is poorly lit.

In the center of the room is a boxing ring. The canvas is decaying and stained by decades of sweat and smoke and the broken dreams of—oh, wait, we already used that description for the bricks. Anyway the canvas is rotting and discolored by tens of years of perspiration and stogey-ash and the busted aspirations of busted men. Or maybe the floor is decomposing like Beethoven in his grave, and is as tainted as the Puritans made Hester Prynne, tainted by night after night and year after year of broken-nosed and brokenhearted men beating each other to a pulp while other men, with hearts as cold as their cash, cheered them on and jeered as the tattered fragments of their dreams splattered like their blood across the fabric of the flooring in this arena to serve a spectacle as gaudy and horrifying (and popular) as those of the Roman Coliseum.

Or maybe the canvas floor is aging gracefully, suffused with the sweat and blood and hopes and dreams of young men. It is carrying these hopes and dreams long after the men themselves have grown old and tired, carrying these hopes and dreams to inspire a new generation of men to train, to hone their skills, to strengthen their bodies and their wills and their intuition, to learn to listen, always, to the muse of the Ring, and in so doing this humble canvas has helped to initiate these men into a brotherhood and tradition and even a form of spirituality that stretches farther back than men can remember, and stretches farther into the future than anyone can guess, leading these humble men into an immortality of sorts, and has done the same for generation after generation of those in attendance, those who witness and also worship through this Sport of Kings.

All of this may or may not have been true a few days ago, but in preparation for the duel the MAWAR folks all headed down to the sperm donation center to collect some dough (the people at the sperm bank wondered why their leader brought with him an illustrated Bible), and used the money to buy another canvas floor for the boxing ring, to replace the old one, which was falling apart.

On the walls of this dimly lit gym are posters advertising some of the greatest fights in history (none of which took place here). Ali versus Frazier. Louis versus Schmelling. Johnson versus Jeffries. Hagler versus Hearns. Jesus versus Temptation. The Temptations versus the Supremes. Rock and Roll versus Disco. St. Augustine versus his unruly penis. Capitalists vanquishing their consciences. Industrialization versus life on Earth.

The members of MAWAR sit on folding chairs, murmuring excitedly and waving cigars. At one side of the ring is Jasmine, the prize, tied to a chair. In the ring is Ezekiel. He wears a garish wrestling outfit with mask, cape, and boots. His huge belt buckle features the MAWAR logo, and "MAWAR" is stenciled crookedly across his chest. He carries a big Bible (the 1976 Bicentennial edition, with an embossed Liberty Bell on the cover) in one hand, and his lucky crucifix in the other.

Facing him is Sam, who is also wearing a wrestling outfit with mask, cape, and boots. Under the cape, he wears a tweed jacket with leather elbow patches. He sports glasses, has a pipe clenched between his teeth, and carries a textbook called *Introduction to Exegetical Thought*.

A referee stands between them. He looks like Uncle Wiggily, and carries a candy-striped cane in one hand, a whistle in the other. He puts the whistle to his mouth, and blows one sharp blast.

The MAWAR men stop their murmuring, and put down their refurbished cigars (after splurging on the canvas they're going to be a little short on cash until they can replenish their precious bodily fluids, so they've been getting refurbished cigars, made from the finest and fattest butts found in the trash cans behind Fat Gordi's Cigar Bar ["Every Tuesday is Ladie's Night! Hey Ladie's, get your fat butts in here! And with our prices you can be sure we're not blowing any smoke up your ass!"]).

Into the room walk four women with highly styled, frosted hair. They make their way to the sidelines, smiling and smiling and smiling. They wear short aprons and tight sweaters with LAWAR appliqued across their chests. Each wears around her neck her second most precious piece of jewelry after her wedding ring: her 12-karat gold hand-scripted pendant reading "Try God." They carry toilet brushes and feather dusters. One of them holds up her arms for attention. The others fall into line, hands on hips.

The first one says, "Ready! Set!"

Jasmine tugs on the arm of Billy Bob, standing next to her. "Who are they?"

Billy Bob says, "Cheerleaders. Duh."

"No, I mean, who are they?"

"They're LAWAR. Ladies Against Women Against Rape."

"But . . . who are they?"

"Our wives."

"Ah."

The LAWAR women jump and wave around their cleaning implements as they perform a cheer. "Gimme a 'G'!"

The men roar, "G!"

"Gimme an 'O'!"

"O!"

"Gimme a 'D'!"

"D!"

"And whattaya got? The One whose name we cannot take in vain! Go, GAWAR!"

"GAWAR?" Jasmine asks.

"Can't you figure out anything? That's God Against Women Against Rape," Billy Bob says.

The women try another cheer afterwards, lustily chanting, "We've got The Spirit, how about you?"

But there are no fans on the other side, with or without The Spirit, to respond, so that one fizzles.

The referee calls them all to attention. He then says to the combatants, "This will be a clean fight. There will be no headbutting, no hitting below the belt, no ad hominem attacks, and, following the rules set forth by Jürgen Habermas, speakers may only assert what they truly believe, and may not dispute a proposition or norm not under discussion without providing a reason for wanting to do so. Further, we have been given specific dispensation from Our Lord and Savior to allow you not to turn the other cheek. And finally, of course, no biting. Do you agree?"

Both fighters nod.

The referee continues, "Return to your corners, and come out swinging. May the best man—by which we mean the most Holy Man of God—win!"

Both fighters retreat to their corners. The leader of MAWAR rings a bell. Both fighters step to toward the center.

Ezekiel lands the first blow by stating, triumphantly, "Deuteronomy 21:11! It says there that when God helps you kick some heathen ass, and you see some really hot chick, you get to take her home to be 'your wife.'"

The MAWAR and LAWAR crowd cheers.

Sam nods thoughtfully.

The cheering grows even louder.

Sam says, "So you're equating rape with marriage?"

The crowd clearly thinks this blow landed directly on Ezekiel's solar plexus, as they fall silent, stunned.

But Ezekiel is unfazed. He says, "Read some books, Four Eyes. Deuteronomy 21:14 answers that one: if she's not a good lay, you can send her packing back to Mommy and Daddy, but can't sell her as a slave. So rape only equals marriage if she's fuckin' hot!"

The referee waves his candy-striped cane and says, "Two points to Ezekiel."

Ezekiel moves in close for a body blow: "Ready for another one? The whole fuckin' story of Genesis 19!"

More cheering.

He pushes home the attack, "Lot lived in . Angels came to town, and them fuckin' sodomites—get it?—wanted to rape them angels, but Lot said no, you can't have them angels. Instead you can have my two daughters. Did Lot pull out any knitting needles? Hell, no, bub. God woulda turned his ass to salt."

Sam looks dazed.

Ezekiel moves in for the knockout punch. "Now let's go back to Deuteronomy, Academic-boy. How about a little Deuteronomy 22 action? The whole fuckin' chapter."

Sam is up against the ropes.

Jasmine shouts, "Do something!"

Ezekiel offers a flurry of verses, "How about the story in Numbers 31, or Second Samuel 12:11–14? Judges 21. You want more, boy? You had enough?"

Sam stutters, "I . . ."

Ezekiel is relentless. His flurry is staggering Sam. Ezekiel says, "There's plenty more where that came from. We got us some Zechariah 14, verses 1 and 2. We got us some . . ."

Sam leans over the ropes and says to Jasmine, "I have a secret weapon at my disposal."

Ezekiel hears him, crows, "Bring it on!"

Sam staggers away from Ezekiel, but becomes more steady as he approaches his corner. After he takes a standing eight count, he regains his composure, sits on his stool, crosses one leg over the other, European style, puffs contemplatively on his empty pipe, then takes the pipe out of his mouth. He looks absent-mindedly at it for a moment, before he begins to speak. "I must reject not only your logic and your sources, but even your epistemology itself. We must begin with the Notion."

Ezekiel says, "Huh," as though hit with a philosophical blow to the gut. Or maybe it makes as little sense to him as it does to anyone else.

Jasmine says, "Your secret weapon is a notion?"

Sam doesn't seem to be worried. "As I'm sure you know, in his *Shorter Logic*, first published in 1830, Hegel wrote that 'The notion is what is mediated through itself and with itself. It is a mistake to imagine that the objects which form the content of our mental ideas come first, and that our subjective agency then supervenes, and by the aforesaid operation of abstraction, and by colligating the points possessed in common by the objects, frames notions of them.' You see how this applies, do you not?"

Ezekiel looks stupefied.

The referee waves his candy-striped cane around briskly and blows his whistle. He says, sharply, "Two points taken away. No Hegel."

Sam doesn't hesitate. He says, "No loss. If we're going to speak of God's support of rape we must speak of the existence of God. For this I prefer Wittgenstein's approach to truth as manifested in his *Tractatus Logico-Philosophicus*, where he stated quite clearly, and, ahem, this is my own modest translation, that according to the nature of truth-operations, in the same way as out of elementary propositions arise their truth functions . . ."

The referee shakes his head to stir himself awake, and has to blow a couple three times on his whistle to get it to make a sort of "piffle" sound. He says, sleepily, "Two more points lost. No Wittgenstein."

Sam continues calmly, patiently, really hitting his academic stride. "Well, then, let us accept that before we can talk of rape, we must talk of the metaphysics, indeed, the metasymbology, of free will. And before we can speak of free will, we must speak of, if I may coin a phrase, metaepistemological exegetic dialecticalism . . ."

Ezekiel is having a hard time standing.

Sam continues, "I'm sure we all know that, as Kierkegaard wrote, 'in the interest of ever more highly specialized deliberation'—and Biblical exegetics are nothing if not specialized—which by forgetting—well, I'll skip over that and dash right to the point where we attain . . ."

Sam looks around, then continues, more and more slowly and quietly, as if to a child falling asleep, ". . . a dubious perfectibility by being able to become anything at all."

There is complete silence in the gym, except for the ticking of a far-off clock, and the slight hiss of steam in the pipes, and the faint sound of distant traffic, and the louder sound of closer traffic, and helicopters flying overhead, and jets taking off from the nearby airport, and the thunderous snoring of Ezekiel and several of the members of MAWAR and LAWAR. Even Uncle Wiggly snores fitfully, leaning on his candy-striped cane.

Sam quietly climbs through the ropes and out of the ring. He tiptoes to Jasmine. With one hand he gently shakes her awake while with his other hand he holds a finger to his lips. She grins as he unties her. They step quietly around the sleeping MAWAR and LAWAR members and out the door. Once outside, they start running.

The sensible response to Jasmine's dramatic rescue is to gather at the house of the most sensible person and eat cake and ice cream. So the core members of the knitting circle and friends gather at Gina's house. Jasmine is hugged by everyone in turn. "Sam did a splendid job at the duel!" she gushes.

Sam blushes and smiles bashfully as Suzie beams with pride. Suzie says, "He was just doing what he does best!"

Gina raises her cake in a toast, "That was the enemy's last hope. They've got nothing left. They're finished. We've won!"

Everyone cheers.

Jasmine leans over to Christine, and says, "And you know, his teeth weren't even really that good."

It is a few days later. Sandy knocks at Brigitte's door. From inside Sandy hears the sounds of Sophie Scholl and the rest of the White Rose Orchestra performing "The Ride of the Valkyries."

Nick peers between the curtains and sees her. He panics,

ducks below the window, hiding.

Sandy calls out to him, "I saw you, Nick. Don't worry, I'm not here to arrest you."

He sheepishly opens the door. Sandy asks how he is.

"I'm going crazy, locked up in here."

She replies, "This is your lucky day. I'm here to tell you that you can come out now."

His eyes widen. He asks, "What about those cops who want to arrest me? Who want to *shoot* me?"

Sandy says, simply, "They're gone."

He raises his eyebrows.

Sandy pantomimes stabbing herself in the heart with a knitting needle. Nick grins.

Sandy grins back. She says, "I'm the highest ranking cop left. In fact, I've used my new authority to shut down the police station. I've turned it into the Community Self-Defense Academy. Our new mission is to arm the community for self-defense, and train everyone in the use of knitting needles. You know, to preserve the peace."

Nick responds, "I love it! And I'm *free!*" He runs outside and dances on the lawn, sort of a combination of a Vienna-style waltz and the Charleston.

Sandy smiles. "Would you like to volunteer at the Academy? We could use someone like you, with your valuable experience of being a Lone Secret Turtle Agent of Death."

Nick corrects her: "That's Undercover Secret Agent Lone Wolf."

"Whatever. Do you want to?"

"I'll come right now!"

Nick skips to her car (a red Corvette) and opens the passenger door.

Brigitte comes to her door and sees Nick leaving. She calls out, "Nick! Where are you—" She stops herself abruptly.

Nick asks, "What, Brigitte?"

She says, "Nothing! Bye! Have fun!"

"I will, thanks!"

Suzie and Sam are on Suzie's bed. They are, if you can believe it, still fully clothed. Except that by now they have at least taken off their socks.

Sam says to Suzie, "I know you *say* you want to. But how do I know that you really absolutely positively want to? How can I be sure you're not just 'allowing' it because you'd feel guilty for rejecting me, or because you want me to be happy even if you aren't, or as a favor, or because you're being kind, or because you're rewarding me for doing the dishes, or for some other bad reason that if I knew about it would be depressing and humiliating?"

She responds, "During this encounter so far, have you heard me sigh, even once, in a burdened sort of way?"

"No."

"Did I say 'I want to make love with you' in the same tone of voice that I use when I say something like, 'Okay, I'll take out the garbage'?"

Sam smiles. "Not exactly."

"Does my mood seem sort of blah, ho-hum, ehhh—or does my voice seem warm and enthusiastic when I say 'I'm mad for you! I adore you! I love your hot delicious body, especially with my arms and legs wrapped around it'?"

"You seem fairly warm and enthusiastic . . . kind of. Can you repeat all that so I can make sure?"

Suzie gives him a playful shove. She says, "Now, to make

this very easy for you, when a basketball player hits a home run to win the Super Bowl, and he runs around with his arms waving, grinning and laughing, can you tell if he's really absolutely positively interested in playing the game, or is he just going through the motions because he doesn't want to hurt the other team's feelings, or because they did the dishes?"

Sam muses, "I think if he kissed the other team in a passionate way, and maybe tore off their uniforms in his eagerness to get as close to them as possible, and licked their ears, then I'd really be absolutely positively sure he wanted to play."

They kiss, and finally the clothes begin to come off. Rather quickly. I do believe they set a U.S. and perhaps a world record for the fastest-ever removal of clothes.

Brigitte is walking toward the cheese factory. Today is Gaperon day, and the smell of cream, peppercorns, and garlic is already making her salivate. She is humming and swinging her tote bag.

She sees people laughing and smiling. She sees couples (of all gender combinations) holding hands, walking, sharing milkshakes with two straws. She sees someone she recognizes from pre-knitting-circle fashion advertisements as a supermodel eating a huge piece of cake. She walks past burned-out porn stores and high-fashion boutiques. She walks past a garbage can that overflows with broken high-heeled shoes. Brigitte smiles and says hello to passersby, and they return her greetings.

Jasmine and Suzie walk along another street, also on their way to the cheese factory. They've never before tasted this particular cheese, but the smell wafting through the city is so good they know they will love it.

In the sunlight the two beautiful young women, filled

with energy and confidence and lofty dreams, shimmer as they always do, from the top of their glossy hair down to the flashes of iridescent color on their toenails. Glittering brightest of all are their happy eyes, as they swing their tote bags of knitting supplies back and forth and chatter together about grand plans, Suzie's boyfriend (who is as adorable as a whole litter of soft baby bunnies), and Jasmine's new girlfriend (well, we're not actually sure if she's her new girlfriend since she hasn't actually called, but she has texted 07734, which after much puzzling, Jasmine discovered spells "hello" upside-down) and they have met online several times and she's the cutest woman in the world (after Suzie and Jasmine herself, of course) who sometimes looks like a gorgeous bird and sometimes a willow tree).

The women pass a building under construction.

A construction worker notices them. He yells, "Hey! Hey!"

They turn, smiling.

Jasmine says, "Yes?"

He points at them, says, "Your yarn . . . it's dragging on the ground!"

Jasmine thanks him, and tucks the yarn back in her bag.

All of the original knitters are at the cheese factory. Nick is also there, as is Marilyn, as is Sandy. A plate of the Gaperon has been left out for all of them, with very plain crackers that don't compete with the exquisitely subtle taste of the cheese. They are eating slowly, savoring each bite.

When they finish this act of worship, they begin to knit.

Brigitte says, "Everything turned out magnificently. It's a happy ending."

Jasmine quickly responds, "For a real happy ending, we need wedding bells. There are *always* wedding bells at the happy ending. From *Cinderella* and *Snow White* to *Bridget Jones's Diary*, wedding bells signify and define *Happy Ending*. You can't have a happy ending without them. Come on, Brigitte and Nick. We're counting on you."

Brigitte says, "I don't hear any wedding bells. Do you hear any wedding bells, Nick?"

Nick puts down the cheese he was nibbling, and gets on one knee. He says to her, "Brigitte, I love you very much. Will you marry me anyway? Will you make us miserable slaves to each other for the rest of our lives?"

Brigitte gets tears in her eyes, and answers, "Oh, my darling! I love you way too much to do that to either one of us. I'd rather get a knitting needle through the heart."

Nick exclaims, "I knew you'd say *no*! This is the moment I've always dreamed of! You've made me the happiest man in the world!" He throws his arms around her.

Brigitte turns to the group and says, "And that's *our* happy ending."

Romantic music swells, white doves fly, and rose petals fall from the sky (or at least the ceiling), as Brigitte and Nick gently kiss.

Abruptly, the music stops. Everyone in the cheese factory notices its absence.

Gina turns to Brigitte. "What do you mean, 'ending'? Okay, we stopped rape. We empowered women. What about the rest?"

Marilyn asks, "The rest?"

Gina answers, "Sure. Now that we're all empowered and everything, what are we going to do with that? The world didn't need rapists. As far as they don't overlap, does the world need CEOs? Politicians? Fast-food restaurants? Fashion magazine publishers? Dictators? Advertising? Industrialists? Priests?

Generals?"

Marilyn whines, in a way that only teenagers can whine, "Mom! Don't you *ever* get tired?"

They all laugh, eat cheese, and continue talking and knitting.

Marilyn, much older now, stands at the front of a classroom.

She is talking to her students. She says, "My mom and her friends didn't set out to change the world. All they wanted to do was make fabulous sweaters. But it led to much more than that. Now we have a beautiful existence. No more rape, no more war, freedom from all the horrors and injustices of capitalism. And, though this is all theoretical to you thus far, even sex is better.

"For now we've put our knitting needles back on the shelf. But we remember where they are, just in case."

ABOUT DERRICK JENSEN

Hailed as the philosopher poet of the ecological movement, Derrick Jensen is the widely acclaimed author of *Endgame, A Language Older than Words*, and *The Culture of Make Believe*, among many others. Jensen's writing has been described as "breaking and mending the reader's heart" (*Publishers Weekly*). His books with PM include: *Truths Among Us: Conversations on Building a New Culture* and the novels *Songs of the Dead* and *Lives Less Valuable*.

Author, teacher, activist, and leading voice of uncompromising dissent, he regularly stirs auditoriums across the country with revolutionary spirit. Jensen holds a degree in mineral engineering physics from the Colorado School of Mines, and has taught at Eastern Washington University and Pelican Bay Prison. He lives in Crescent City, California.

ABOUT STEPHANIE MCMILLAN

Stephanie McMillan self-syndicates the award-winning editorial cartoon *Code Green*, and creates the daily comic strip *Minimum Security* for Universal Uclick.

She has a book of comics journalism, *The Beginning of the American Fall* (Seven Stories Press, 2012); a comic strip collection, *Attitude Presents Minimum Security* (NBM, 2005); plus two other books co-created with Derrick Jensen: a graphic novel, *As the World Burns: 50 Simple Things You Can Do to Stay in Denial* (Seven Stories Press, 2007); and a children's book, *Mischief in the Forest* (PM Press/Flashpoint, 2010).

She is also an organizer for the anti-capitalist/anti-imperialist collective One Struggle (onestrugglesouthflorida.wordpress. com). She lives in Fort Lauderdale, Florida.

FRIENDS OF PM PRESS

These are indisputably momentous times—the financial system is melting down globally and the Empire is stumbling. Now more than ever there is a vital need for radical ideas.

Since its founding in 2007—on a mere shoestring—PM Press has risen to the formidable challenge of publishing and distributing knowledge and entertainment for the struggles ahead. With over 200 releases to date, we have published an impressive and stimulating array of literature, art, music, politics, and culture. Using every available medium, we've succeeded in connecting those hungry for ideas and information to those putting them into practice.

Friends of PM allows you to directly help impact, amplify, and revitalize the discourse and actions of radical writers, filmmakers, and artists. It provides us with a stable foundation from which we can build upon our early successes and provides a much-needed subsidy for the materials that can't necessarily pay their own way. You can help make that happen—and receive every new title automatically delivered to your door once a month—by joining as a Friend of PM Press. And, we'll throw in a free T-Shirt when you sign up.

Here are your options:

* $25 a month: Get all books and pamphlets plus 50% discount on all webstore purchases

* $40 a month: Get all PM Press releases (including CDs and DVDs) plus 50% discount on all webstore purchases

* $100 a month: Superstar - Everything plus PM merchandise, free downloads, and 50% discount on all webstore purchases

For those who can't afford $25 or more a month, we're introducing Sustainer Rates at $15, $10 and $5. Sustainers get a free PM Press t-shirt and a 50% discount on all purchases from our website.

Your Visa or Mastercard will be billed once a month, until you tell us to stop. Or until our efforts succeed in bringing the revolution around. Or the financial meltdown of Capital makes plastic redundant. Whichever comes first.

PO Box 23912
Oakland, CA 94623
www.pmpress.org

PM Press was founded at the end of 2007 by a small collection of folks with decades of publishing, media, and organizing experience. PM Press co-conspirators have published and distributed hundreds of books, pamphlets, CDs, and DVDs. Members of PM have founded enduring book fairs, spearheaded victorious tenant organizing campaigns, and worked closely with bookstores, academic conferences, and even rock bands to deliver political and challenging ideas to all walks of life. We're old enough to know what we're doing and young enough to know what's at stake.

We seek to create radical and stimulating fiction and non-fiction books, pamphlets, t-shirts, visual and audio materials to entertain, educate and inspire you. We aim to distribute these through every available channel with every available technology - whether that means you are seeing anarchist classics at our bookfair stalls; reading our latest vegan cookbook at the café; downloading geeky fiction e-books; or digging new music and timely videos from our website.

PM Press is always on the lookout for talented and skilled volunteers, artists, activists and writers to work with. If you have a great idea for a project or can contribute in some way, please get in touch.

ABOUT FLASHPOINT PRESS

Flashpoint Press was founded by Derrick Jensen to ignite a resistance movement. Our planet is under serious threat from industrial civilization, with its consumption of biotic communities, production of greenhouse gases and environmental toxins, and destruction of human rights and human-scale cultures around the globe. This system will not stop voluntarily, and it cannot be reformed.

Flashpoint Press believes that the Left has severely limited its strategic thinking, by insisting on education, lifestyle change, and techno-fixes as the only viable and ethical options. None of these responses can address the scale of the emergency now facing our planet. We need both a serious resistance movement and a supporting culture of resistance that can inspire and protect frontline activists. Flashpoint embraces the necessity of all levels of action, from cultural work to militant confrontation. We also intend to win.

FLASHPOINT PRESS
CRESCENT CITY, CALIFORNIA

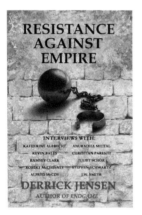

Resistance Against Empire
$20 (e-Book $10)

A scathing indictment of U.S. domestic and foreign policy, this collection of interviews gathers insights from 10 of today's most experienced and knowledgeable activists. Whether it's Ramsey Clark describing the long history of military invasion, Alfred McCoy detailing the relationship between CIA activities and the increase in the global heroin trade, Stephen Schwartz reporting the obscene costs of nuclear armaments, or Katherine Albrecht tracing the horrors of the modern surveillance state, this investigation of global governance is sure to inform, engage, and incite readers.

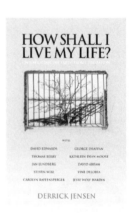

How Shall I Live My Life? On Liberating the Earth from Civilization
$20 (e-Book $10)

In this collection of interviews, Derrick Jensen discusses the destructive dominant culture with ten people who have devoted their lives to undermining it. These activists and philosophers, including Carolyn Raffensperger, Thomas Berry, Kathleen Dean Moore and Vine Deloria, bravely present a few of the endless forms that resistance can and must take.

Truths Among Us: Conversations on Building a New Culture $20

Derrick Jensen interviews, among others, acclaimed sociologist Stanley Aronowitz, poet and peacemaker Luis Rodriguez, and the brilliant Judith Herman, who helps us understand the psychology of trauma. Paul Stamets reveals the power of fungi, and writer Richard Drinnon reminds us that our spiritual paths need not be narrowed by the limiting mythologies of Western civilization. The brave voices in this book seek to help us acknowledge the values we know are right, and to act on them.

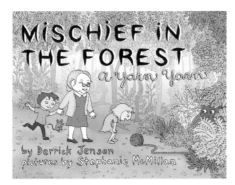

Mischief in the Forest: A Yarn Yarn (with Stephanie McMillan) $14.95

Grandma Johnson lives alone in the forest and loves to knit sweaters and mittens for her grandchildren. One day, her mischievous forest neighbors reveal themselves in a delightfully colorful fashion. This picture book inspires both young and old to connect with one's surroundings and embrace the role of good neighbors with the rest of the natural world, whether in the city or in the forest.

Lives Less Valuable
$18 (e-Book $10)
In the heart of a city, a river is dying, children have cancer, and people are burning with despair. From the safe distance that wealth buys, a corporation called Vexcorp counts these lives as another expense on a balance sheet. But that distance is about to collapse. Derrick Jensen has written a novel as compelling as it is necessary: With our planet under serious threat, Malia's decisions face us all.

Songs of the Dead
$20 (e-Book $10)
In this thriller, a serial killer stalks the streets of Spokane, acting out a misogynist script from the dark heart of this culture. Across town, a writer has spent his life tracking the reasons—political, psychological, spiritual—for the sadism of modern civilization. And through the grim nights, Nika, a trafficked woman, tries to survive the grinding violence of prostitution. Their lives, and the forces propelling them, are about to collide.

Now This War Has Two Sides [double CD] $19.99

Examining the premises of his controversial work *Endgame*, as well as core elements of his groundbreaking book *The Culture of Make Believe*, this two hour lecture and discussion offers both a perfect introduction for newcomers and additional insight for those already familiar with Derrick Jensen's work.

END:CIV: Resist or Die (directed and produced by Franklin Lopez) [DVD] $19.95

Based in part on Derrick Jensen's bestselling book *Endgame*, *END:CIV* asks: "If your homeland was invaded by aliens who cut down the forests, poisoned the water and air, and contaminated the food supply, would you resist?" Backed by Jensen's narrative, *END:CIV* features interviews with more than 20 leading activists and thinkers.

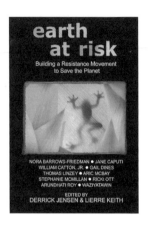

Earth at Risk: Building a Resistance Movement to Save the Planet $20

Earth at Risk is an annual conference featuring environmental thinkers and activists who are willing to ask the hardest questions about the seriousness of our situation. This book collects Derrick Jensen's interviews of Arundhati Roy, William Catton, Jr., Rikki Ott, Thomas Linzey, Gail Dines, Jane Caputi, Waziyatawin, Aric McBay, Stephanie McMillan, Lierre Keith, and Nora Barrows-Friedman.

Earth at Risk: Building a Resistance Movement to Save the Planet [DVD] $19.95

This film contains Derrick Jensen's interviews of Arundhati Roy, Thomas Linzey, Waziyatawin, Aric McBay, Stephanie McMillan, and Lierre Keith.

The Vegetarian Myth: Food, Justice, and Sustainability, by Lierre Keith $20

Agriculture is a relentless assault against the Earth. If we are to save this planet, our food must be an act of repair, coming from inside communities rather than imposed across them. Part memoir, part nutritional primer, and part political manifesto, this book will challenge everything you thought you knew abuot food politics.

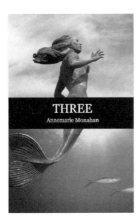

Three, by Annemarie Monahan $16.95

The founder of a radical feminist community, a doctor haunted by a past lover, a struggling mother. In this novel, these three women lead very different, yet parallel lives. As they converge, we realize what it is that connects them: they were all once the same seventeen-year-old girl on an April morning, wondering if she would be brave.

Calling All Heroes: A Manual for Taking Power, by Paco Ignacio Taibo II $12

The idealism of grassroots reform and the reality of revolutionary failure are at the center of this speculative novel. In Mexico City, after the government's massacre of civilians in violent repression of the 1968 student movement, Nestor, a journalist and former activist, lies recovering from a knife wound. In his fevered state, he collects memories of past events and summons heroes of his youth such as Sherlock Holmes and Wyatt Earp to launch a new uprising.

Revolutionary Women: A Book of Stencils, by Queen of the Neighbourhood $12

A radical feminist history and street art resource for inspired readers! This book combines short biographies with striking and usable stencil images of thirty women—activists, anarchists, feminists, freedom-fighters, and visionaries.

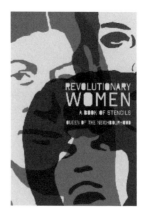

Vida, by Marge Piercy $20

Originally published in 1979, *Vida* bookends the optimistic 1960s with the tale of activist Vida Asche, a star of the antiwar movement who faced the choice between working within the system and taking radical action. Having chosen the latter, she now struggles to survive underground during the subsequent political ebb and loss of interest among the former supporters of her cause.

The Wild Girls, by Ursula K. Le Guin $12

From the brilliant science fiction author is this Nebula winning story of two captive "dirt children" in a society of swords and silk, whose determination to attain justice leads to a violent and loving end. The book also contains Le Guin's scorching *Harper's* essay "Staying Awake While We Read," which demolishes the pretentions of corporate publishing and the basic assumptions of capitalism as well.